MW01442547

THE PULL

Ralph Nathanial Wells

Copyright © 2018 Ralph Nathanial Wells
All rights reserved
First Edition

PAGE PUBLISHING, INC.
New York, NY

First originally published by Page Publishing, Inc. 2018

ISBN 978-1-64214-685-1 (Paperback)
ISBN 978-1-64214-687-5 (Hardcover)
ISBN 978-1-64214-686-8 (Digital)

Printed in the United States of America

CONTENTS

The Discovery

Chapter 1: A Normal Human Being 7
Chapter 2: My Mother's House: House of Magic 14
Chapter 3: A Boy and a Kitchen 19
Chapter 4: A Daughter's Love 25
Chapter 5: A Very Unusual Art Gallery 28
Chapter 6: The Princess and the Guest Quarters 32
Chapter 7: Sister Witch and Brother Magneto 38
Chapter 8: An Unidentified Flying Object 42
Chapter 9: The Attic and the Shoebox 48
Chapter 10: The College Student and the Professor 54
Chapter 11: Remembering My Mother and My Father 61
Chapter 12: A Broken Promise 69
Chapter 13: Letters to Her Daughter 73

The First Ray: Earth—Survival or Fear!

Chapter 14: The Story of Wahketsi Begins 83
Chapter 15: Chief Iahoo Speaks at Red Clay 87
Chapter 16: The Story of the Eagle and the Owl 93
Chapter 17: Wahketsi Disobeys Her Father 99
Chapter 18: The Gold Rush and the Cotton Gin 103
Chapter 19: The Warrior and the Ghost Spirit 106
Chapter 20: Captain Buford "Bumpy" Hastings 114
Chapter 21: Daughter of Twelve Moons and First Sun of
　　　　　　 Cherokee 121

Chapter 22: Vision of the Moon Goddess 127
Chapter 23: Good Meets Evil 130
Chapter 24: Wahketsi Must Go to the Paint Rock 139
Chapter 25: The Chess Match Begins 145
Chapter 26: The Makings of a Good Soldier 152
Chapter 27: The Pilgrimage 156
Chapter 28: A Planned Attack 161
Chapter 29: Where Their Paths Crossed 168
Chapter 30: The Paint Rock and the Moon Lady 172
Chapter 31: The Story of the Eagle and the Owl Explained 179
Chapter 32: The Anointing 186
Chapter 33: A Hidden Secret in the Forest 193
Chapter 34: Wahketsi: The New Star 201

THE DISCOVERY

Zep Tepi—in the void of time and space, the soul's experience programs by those who move from reality to reality. Those of the first time.

When I came too, I was already standing on my feet, and I immediately realized that I was being held tight by someone with tremendous strength. The more I struggled to get free, the more in vain my efforts seemed. I twisted and turned so I could see the form of this behemoth that refused to release me from its powerful grip, but nothing made any sense.

The figure that has me paralyzed by its brute force appeared to be that of a woman. Not just any woman but a very beautiful woman! And, somehow, she reminded me of my mother! The room also looked very familiar. Yes! It's my bedroom! Who or whatever was holding me was in my house!

Fear was now causing me to tremble to the point that my entire body was shaking. And then there was also this odd omnipresence in the room which felt as if I was being watched by more than one pair of eyes. It added a surreal feeling to the panic and anxiousness of the moment.

Words were being spoken, but I couldn't understand what's being said. I heard the words being repeated over and over, until finally I realized that I was being asked a question. Then all of a sudden, and without any commands from me, I felt my mouth begin to move, and I heard words come out of my mouth that I had no knowledge of their meaning. I hear myself say, "$OE + MC_2 = CO$!"

Then I woke up!

CHAPTER 1

A Normal Human Being

The story I have to tell will be, without any doubt, the strangest and the most bizarre you've ever heard. I'm still having trouble myself with the realization that I'm actually putting down on paper these unnatural events which began during my early teenage years and continue at the present. These events themselves, which were of such abnormality, I have yet to, after all these years, reconcile the facts of them in my own head. Even now it is not without great trepidation that I am attempting to do so. The fact that it had been years since the first of these occurrences took placed led me to falsely assume that what I had experienced that cool summer night of long ago, while asleep in my bed, was just the delirium of a youthful mind.

Certainly, the one person I shared my secret about that night also assured me that it was just the results of an overly active imagination and that it must all had been just a very bad dream. It is one thing, however, to rationalize away the uncertainty of what materializes during the darkest haunting hours of the night as just a dream. But it is quite another thing to attempt to do the same when the supposed dreams starts occurring in broad daylight while one is wide awake and again on a public street while driving in your car!

So I will tell my unbelievable story in spite of the reluctance I may have in exposing the deep recesses of my present state of mind. But I'm going to tell this story the only way I know how—truthfully! What I write here are the events that actually happened to me, and I will tell them exactly the way they occurred. It will be up to everyone else to either accept what I have to say or to reject my story. Either way, I would have fulfilled my obligation to mankind. I would have given the warning that there is more to this world than what we see. So when I say that this story is strange, I'm only trying to be considerate of how much I think your mind can handle. This is actually an unfathomably amazing tale to tell, and your mind will be stretched in ways you can't even now imagine with what I have to say.

I'm not a writer. These are not the hands of one who sits all day at a computer and dream up fantastic stories to write about like some fiction writer would do. No, that's not how I make my living. I design, build, and create things that once didn't exist. And I've been doing that for over twenty years. So that's all I know how to do. Writing is just not something I do. But this wasn't my idea, at least not initially. I want to repeat that—this was not my idea!

I don't want there to be any misunderstandings of why I decided to write my story: Try to think of the most embarrassing and private moments in your life, your most well-kept secrets, anything that you would be afraid to let someone else know about you. Now imagine that somehow you were required to expose those secrets to complete strangers. Oh, yeah! Don't forget that if you don't reveal everything regardless to how insignificant it may seem, this lifelong nightmare you've been having would continue. Would you be eager to take on such a project? The idea itself would become a nightmare! It would be a living hell!

That's the real life I'm living and have been living for a very long time now. So honestly, for me, I don't feel I have much of a choice because my nightmare is real! What began, for me, as the most unusual imaginings possible is now flesh and blood, lives and breathes, and is threatening my very sanity, my very existence! And yet, in spite of all my claims to you of my saneness, I'm sure, just as all my friends have deserted me, you too will have ill thoughts of me when I'm done. You will, no doubt, make the very rational and intelligent decision that they all made. They were convinced of my delusional state and my need for psychiatric treatment. It would be the only sensible conclusion to come to, for if you were to accept any part of the narrative I'm to put forth in these writings, you would be disavowing all you have come to know and understand. You would be, in essence, condemning the very society and world we live in today.

Now I ask you! Would any sane person surrender all their values, beliefs, and traditions so readily? Or would some extreme form of altered reality be needed to bring about such a complete capitulation? Please then, don't assume that I didn't consider every alternative possibility before I consented to fill these pages, the contents of which, I'm sure, will appear to be the ravings of a madman with the dictations that were being given to me. Like most Americans, I obey and defend the constitution of these United States of America! And my father fought and died for this country! Even if that were not the case, I, too, cherish life and relish the idea of freedom just like all other living creatures. The true mystery of life shouldn't be the fact that we have it but rather the fact that we fight so hard to keep it. Self-preservation is the strongest drive of all living beings.

Therefore, as I'm sure you can imagine, I didn't just go quietly into the night, as it were. I resisted, I challenged, and I fought back against this nemesis who have plagued my life like a rusty nail protruding through the sole of my shoe. So before you mount your high horse and look upon me with judgmental eyes, remember, "There are forms of coercion that are more frightening then the threat of death itself," and "Don't hate the messenger!" Especially the one who has been predestined, it would seem, to be a cursed oracle. Instead, pray that what you read here are, indeed, the words of a lunatic. Should any truth reside in these pages, it may ultimately establish my sanity, but it would also, at the same time, be the precursor for a radical change to the world as it exist today.

My name is Raphael Wellington. My friends call me Obi. It was because of the first incident, of which I speak, that directly lead to my receiving this nickname. How little did I understand then the significance of that one fated moment. I should first tell you that I'm a normal human being. I live a normal life with my wife and two kids in Northern Virginia. I have a small construction company, and my wife, Birdie, is a chiropractor. All things considered, I had a very normal and happy childhood. I attended public schools, got good grades, and I loved playing sports like most young boys. Every Sunday, my mother saw to it that my sister, Rachael, and I attended Sunday school. Most of the time, we were even required to stay after for church service. While my friends got to play all day on their second day of freedom from school, I had to learn about Noah's Ark, Abraham and Isaac, Moses and the Ten Commandments, and all the rest of the major and minor prophets of the Old Testament.

But freedom finally came my way one day. It was after my twelfth birthday. My mother came into my room while I was getting ready for another boring Sunday. She said it was time for us to have a talk about our family—that I needed to know certain things about our history. But it wasn't until she got to the part about my no longer having to attend church that my attention became focus on the conversation. After explaining to me all the virtues of being a faithful servant of God, she, in the most gross miscalculation of her motherhood—however sincere her intentions may have been—freed me from my shackles. Stating that she now expected me to start making mature decisions for myself, and that from now on, it would be my choice whether or not I attended church service.

It felt, at that precise moment, she had just opened the door to my cage. Once the door to the birdcage has been opened, no one should expect the bird to return when there is a whole forest to explore. Yes! That day! I felt I knew why the caged bird sang! It wanted to be free to fly! It wanted to soar! And soar I did. I never willingly attended church service again. In fact, it would be many years before my feet would walk across the threshold of a church door.

For my mother, this was an unexpected blow, which I don't think she ever fully recovered from. The conversation we had that early Sunday morning was her attempt to help me understand our family's history. How and why she felt it was important for me to understand how the tradition of attending church came about for our family wasn't clear to me at all! What she revealed to me that day, however, about my family should have caused a paused in me before I made such a rash and hasty decision. It would have, I think, for most people. But not for me. I just wanted to go play with my friends. Of course, now I feel I may have been too young to fully grasp the significance of what she was trying to relay to me. As I start this writing, I'm now forty years old, and it's only now that the conversation of that day is beginning to have importance for me.

That conversation was my mother's attempt to tell me some unspoken secret about my family's history. That day, I think now, was meant to be a chance for me to gain some insight into what was to come. Why I would later in life find myself in the predicament that now confronts me. Why I would be the one chosen to bear the burden of the curse that has plagued my family for generations. But I didn't understand that then; as I said, I didn't pay much attention to what was being told to me. All I heard my mother say was I didn't have to attend church anymore.

What first caused my recollection of this conversation I had with my mother that long time ago was when Rachael and I went to our childhood home to start moving my mother's things out. She passed away a year ago, and we wanted to finally start moving on with our lives. We grew up in a two-story house in a modestly influential neighborhood in Fairfax County, and we agreed that we would meet each other back there after work. Now after work for me meant that I would leave directly from my job to go to my mother's house. For my sister, after work meant that she would first go home and change into other clothes before she would come to the house.

My sister, even though she would deny it, in many ways is just like my mother. For her, the idea of packing boxes in the same clothes she worked in that day was unthinkable. With my sister, everything must have a certain order to it. There are clothes for work, clothes for important occasions like church and going out, clothes for relaxation and play, and clothes for packing boxes and moving—which is all fine and dandy; but for some reason, the idea that she could have packed her moving clothes and took them to work with her was just as equally unthinkable.

To bring clothes that she would use for packing boxes to her job was somehow, for her, breaking some rule of proximity. The clothes that were for work were for work only, and the clothes for moving were for moving only, and the two should never meet. In her mind, the different areas of your life are supposed to be kept separate and not come in contact with each other. She said something about, "Never combine the energy of one place with the energy of another place."

This was just one of her many strange quirks along with UFOs, aliens, Bigfoot, ghosts, burning candles, Wicca, Chaldean numerology, tarot cards, astrology, the lunar cycle, and who knows what else. Why, once she even contacted the Naval Observatory just to make sure she had the correct dates for the days of equal day and equal night. What could possibly be so important? Oh! Did I mention that she is an elementary school teacher? She's apparently a very good teacher because she has received many awards from her school board. Maybe believing in all that junk keeps her mind young so she can help shape young impressionable minds. Who knows for sure? She's my sister, and I love her along with all her strange ideas. Besides, she's the only one that has known me all my life and hasn't abandoned me.

Anyway, since she was the one who had the keys and the garage door opener, all I could do was to just sit and wait in my company work van for her to get there. By the time she finally pulled up into the driveway in her little red Ford Escort, it had already started to get dark. I thought it best not to mention that I had been sitting there for over an hour waiting for her. I also knew that the thought would have never occurred to her that it was a little selfish to have someone wait while she went all the way home to change clothes. But to mention it would have only made her defensive because she feels her way of doing things is normal.

So I simply asked, "How was your day?"

But you must remember one thing when it comes to my sister: she spends all her day talking to very small minors, and she seldom has the opportunity to have a prolonged adult conversation. So all day long, this need to converse intelligently is slowly building up inside her like drops of water slowly filling a bucket until they reach the brim. Then the urge to empty this bucket becomes so strong that the first adult person who is foolish enough to engage her in a conversation will have this entire pent-up frustration of the day pour out all over them. So I braced myself to be saturated by the words to come.

"My day," she repeated. "Do you really want to know how I spent my day, Raphael, or is this just you, again, pretending to have an interest in what a teacher has to go through nowadays, trying to teach innocent little children that come from single-family homes or where both parents work all day? Is that really what you want to hear from me?"

Wow, she said all that in one breath, and she called me by my proper first name. I know she's had a very hard day when that happens because she only uses my first name when she is irritated with me.

So I thought I would attempt to soften the mood by interjecting, "Yeah, but, sis, we came from a single family home too."

"Raphael," she countered with vehemence, "not at such an early age as these kids. We were a little bit older when Dad died, and even then, Mom never left the house until we were off to school, and she always made sure to be home by the time we got home. For some of these kids, from the time they get up in the morning until it's time for dinner in the evening, they haven't even seen their parents all day. They wake up all alone in the house to dress themselves, fix themselves a cold bowl of cereal for breakfast, then take their books, leave out the house, and lock the door behind them. Then they walk to where the school bus picks them up. They do all of this all by themselves every day—all alone, Raphael! All alone!"

"Well, sis," was my feeble attempt to end the conversation, "this is the latch-key kid's generation, you know?"

"That's good, Raphael, that's very good! Sum up all of life's problems with another one of your world famous clichés. Latch-key kids, who even says that! People don't even say that anymore. Where have you been hiding, Obi, under a rock?" She lets out a big laugh, and slowly, I start laughing as well because I know her laughter means the bucket is finally empty!

CHAPTER 2

My Mother's House: House of Magic

Once we were inside the house and standing in the doorway, we both looked at each other with that "of course" look on our faces. Even though I had tried to make sure I visited my mother at least a few times a month, and my sister visited her just about daily, we were always impressed how meticulous my mother was at keeping everything in an immaculate condition and how she always had everything in each room arranged perfectly. The house still looked as if someone was living there. For my sister and me, this was the first time we had been back in the house together since my mother's funeral. Birdie wanted everyone to come to our place after the funeral, so she made all the preparations and did all the cooking for the family and the friends who wanted to pay their last respect.

Standing in my mother's house again, with everything inside the house appearing to be in the exact same place as I remembered them growing up, it immediately caused all my childhood memories to flood my mind. We were standing just inside the doorway in the foyer, which had soft cream white marble tiles laid down in an area of about seven feet wide and close to twelve feet long. From there we could look directly into a living room which had perfect symmetrically arranged furniture. The first thing one sees was the luscious creamy ivory color sofa, which as small kids we were never allowed to sit on. Standing on both sides of the sofa were two deep mahogany lamp tables; sitting on top of them were two Tiffany Mother of Pearl lamps that were speckled with mahogany square

THE PULL

shape pieces of glass and each had ivory-colored lampshades on top of them. Perpendicular to the lamp tables, forming a U-shape, were two matching ivory-colored loveseat sofas as well.

In the middle of the sofa and the love seats was a very strangely designed coffee table. It was about half the width of the sofa and nearly as long as the love seats. The coffee table's stand was also of a deep dark mahogany wood with elaborately intricate carvings of African animals on the four arms that acted as supports protruding up from the center of base. These arms, which curved out and up from the base and then curved back over at the top so that the head of each animal was facing away from the table, made the stand almost appear to be some outlandish four armed octopus.

Resting on the four arms of this magnificent work of art was a very beautiful, glossy smoke glass square-shaped table top. Although it was practically impossible to notice with the naked eye—the glass table, using a very unique method of glass working—was formed with a curve that would allow for anyone sitting within the square formed by the seating arrangement of the three sofas to actually see their own reflection coming up from the table. My mother said this table was a rare find—so rare that she didn't think there was another one exactly like it in the whole world. She said she discovered it in a small furniture shop in Sierra Leone on the west coast of Africa where, she reminded me, the mahogany tree grows.

The shop owner told her that the most finely crafted mahogany furniture comes from that part of the world. He then went on to explain the purpose of the table's unusual design. The four arms of the table represented the four directions, and the animals represented the kingdoms of man that would come from these directions. Most noticeably, and clearly as you can see, he began his narration, the focal point of the stand is the arm carved in the image of the great African lion.

The curvature of the arm forms the curvature of the back of the lion in a sitting position with two wings on its back. The lion represented the greatness of the ancient Egyptian kingdom. Most of its secrets are now lost to our civilization, he indicated with some sense of pride as I recall my mother mentioning as she recounted this story to me. The two wings represent the two kingdoms of this great ancient empire. So, he continued to explain, the lion represents the east. The opposite arm is carved in the image of a leopard in an identical sitting position facing the opposite direction. Strong and powerful is the leopard, but just as the setting sun is not as powerful as the rising sun, the leopard is not as powerful as the lion, and the kingdom that followed after the great dynastic period of Ancient Egypt was also not as strong. The leopard represents the west.

Next sits the cheetah, which was carved having four wings of a bird on its back. The speed of the cheetah and the wings of a bird represent how swiftly this kingdom would take the knowledge of Egypt around the world. Therefore, the cheetah represents the south. Lastly is the carving of the strangest animal of all—it had the body of a cheetah, the feet of a leopard, and the mouth of a lion. It represents the kingdom that would combine all the three elements of the first kingdoms to form a great kingdom. This animal represents the north. From these four directions (kingdoms) come all the souls of mankind.

Then he explained the purpose of the black glass. The glass top represents the ocean or the underworld. If a person couldn't resist staring back at their reflection coming from the glass (underworld) top, then they were filled with vanity and their soul belonged to the kingdom of man, and it would be trapped in the underworld. If a person managed not to stare back at their own reflection, then their soul didn't succumb to the temptations of mankind, and their reflection (soul) would transcend their physical existence. This is the story my mother told me and my sister about the reason for the strange design of the table, which she said came directly from the lips of the man who made the table himself. If I'm not mistaken, my mother said the shop owner even said the table had a name. He called it "The Judgment Day Table."

I don't know if my mother actually believed any of that story, at least I don't think she did, but that story left a powerful impression on my sister and me. We were always too afraid to get close enough to the table to look into the glass. While I was standing there staring, from a very safe distance, at this apocalyptic table, my mind some-

THE PULL

how recalled an incident from my very early childhood that I had completely forgotten all about. I could not have been much older than first-grade age, maybe just six or seven.

A friend and I were playing in the house while my mother prepared lunch for us. I was able, in some way or another I can't remember how now, to get him to go into the living room and look into the glass table. He went over and just stood there gazing into the glass with the look of the most profound amazement and disbelief that I had ever seen before. Even until this very day, I don't think I've ever seen such an incredulous look on a person's face. I remembered having an irresistible urge to go see what he was staring at.

What we two little boys saw, long before there were any such things as an in-home computer—desktop or laptop—was not our reflections staring back at us but a moving scene of people dressed in what appeared to be faraway ancient African-looking clothing living in what I can only now say appeared to be houses made of sandstone. The women were dressed in very bright and colorful outfits, and they were carrying baskets on their heads, and the men were mostly dressed in tan trousers and tan shirt tops that went down nearly to their ankles.

They were also wearing turbans on their heads, and they had sandals on their feet. Some of them were riding on the backs of elephants. The sun seemed to be extremely bright; you could almost feel how hot it felt on the skin of these people as they went about their day. All the people were very dark; they were all as black as night! There was greenery and beauty everywhere and water appeared to be in abundance. Off in the distance, there appeared to be two mountains standing side by side.

I tell you this actually happened to us when we looked into the glass of that table, and we were awestruck and petrified for several moments. Then, without saying a word, we both ran into the kitchen to tell my mother what we just saw. She immediately stopped what she was doing and hurried into the living room to investigate our story. I don't know for sure if she saw anything or not when see looked into the smoky glass because when she turned to look back at us, she had an expression on her face that I had never seen before.

I didn't recognize what, I now believe, was fear on my mother's face. She said nothing. She made no comment whatsoever. We were told to never go near the table again.

My friend had to go home, and I was to go without lunch that day as punishment. I never saw this friend again. He never came back to my house to play with me, and I can't even remember his name, but now I do remember one thing—that was the first weird experience of my life. How could I have so completely forgotten it? When I think back now, without the crushing awareness of the fear I experienced that day, that place seemed like it was an amazing and wonderful place to live. Also, something else that seemed strange now that I think back—in spite of the extreme temperature, all the people seemed to be very happy!

Once I became old enough not to fear old wives' tales (well, that's not exactly true; I've always had, and still do, an innate fear of that table), which was around the time I reached middle school age, my mind had shifted to the subject of girls, and I used to love inviting girls over after school so they could walk past the glass table in their short skirts. Well, what else would the mind of a young teenage boy think to do with a highly reflective surface? (What? I said I'm going to be honest.) But now, I only wish I could have known not to be so dismissive with things I didn't fully understand.

One thing was for sure, though—the table was always the centerpiece of conversation when my mother had guests over. And it was one of my mother's most treasured mementos from her travels with my father. All the furniture in this living room sits on an off-white carpet with matching drapes that covered the entire wall directly behind the main sofa. The carpet and the drapes served to exquisitely accent each piece of furniture in the room. Visually, just standing there looking into this room, I finally realized how incredible this sight is to behold. But as a small child, you can't appreciate such beauty. The only thought I remembered having was how much trouble we got in when my mother would catch us playing in there.

CHAPTER 3

A Boy and a Kitchen

To the left of the front double doors, just as you pass the coat closet and the built-into-the-floor fish aquarium, was the entrance into the kitchen. Yes, my mother actually had a fish aquarium that looked more like a miniature pond, with running water and everything, built right into the foyer floor. The smooth round white rocks that started from the wall on one side of this pond-shape aquarium formed a semicircle around the pond until it reached the wall again on the other side of the aquarium, and they were the only barrier that kept you from stepping into the water.

When I was a kid with the imagination of a child, I used to imagine that the wall was a line that divided the circle straight down the middle creating two sections, with one half of the pond in the foyer and the other half in the kitchen. It was so vivid in my mind that I almost expected to see the other half of the pond when I entered into the kitchen. Fortunately, once my mother was hospitalized, I had the foresight to drain the aquarium and give the goldfish to Rachael. Then I covered and sealed it with the glass enclosure my mother would never use. Of course, when she returned home, she was not just a little disappointed with my actions, but I didn't think that it would have been a good idea for her to be doing any bending down, which the up keep of this aquarium frequently required, after her breast cancer surgery.

It seems strange now, but standing there looking into the kitchen, I suddenly remembered all those times I stood at that kitchen stove with tears in my eyes from being so angry because my mother made sure my sister and I learned how to cook. When you enter what I used to consider the torture chamber, to your left is the dinette area with a large round cherry oak table surrounded with four very comfortable light-brown leather chairs that moved on wheels. My mother was always very proud of her design ideas, so of course she knew the name for the light-brown color of the chairs. She said it was called desert sand.

In this area, beginning to the left of the entrance and moving down the wall for about seven feet until it forms an L-shape with the left wall of the kitchen, were a lot of floor cabinets and shelves for storage made from the same Cherry Oak wood. The dinette area also served as my mother's office, and it was the center for where all homework was to be done. I remembered all the homework that we had to do sitting at that table while under her very watchful eyes. From the time we were in elementary school until we were in high school, my mother made us do our homework sitting at that table so she could make sure it got done. Perhaps you're beginning to understand why I had such strong feelings of dislike toward this kitchen.

The dinette area occupied a space of about ten feet by seven feet in the overall design of the kitchen. Protruding out immediately after the dinette area was a waist-high, two-foot wide peninsula that acted as a partition between the two areas. On the dinette side, the peninsula had shelving running back to the wall, and on the kitchen side, it had floor cabinets. The hunter green countertop, which was rounded at the exposed edge of the peninsula, appeared to be one continuous piece of solid granite that covered the top of all the floor cabinets along the left wall of the kitchen. This, of course, was impossible, but it was a testament to the fine craftsmanship of the granite top.

On the peninsula and cut out right through the granite was the double stainless steel kitchen sink. Starting at the peninsula on the kitchen side, the countertop continued down the left wall of the kitchen, for about another seven feet until it turned back into the kitchen making a second L-shape on the far end wall of the kitchen. On that part of the counter was the built-in six-burner stove top, also cut out through the granite, with cherry oak cabinets above and below.

The left wall of the kitchen also had three huge single-pane windows that were each at least four feet wide by six feet tall that started just above the granite backsplash and went almost to the ceiling. Two windows were in the dinette area and one was in the kitchen area. This allowed for plenty of sunlight to penetrate completely into the entire kitchen and dinette areas during the day. But unlike any glass windows I've ever seen, these windows began to tint as they received less and less sunlight until the tint was so dark that someone standing outside could not look inside once it was night. I have no idea where my mother found tinted glass that reacted the opposite way tinted glass was supposed to.

On the right wall of the kitchen, and also starting at the entrance, were two built-into-the-wall refrigeration units. The double-door upright freezer, which came right after a two-foot-wide floor-to-ceiling cabinet, was separated from the refrigerator by a six foot row of cherry oak floor cabinets with a recessed hunter green granite countertop between them. This made the refrigerator actually be in the kitchen area while the freezer was located on the part of the wall that was in the dinette area. Both the refrigerator and the freezer, however, had the cherry oak wood face finish, so they appeared to be a part of the cabinets and not appliances at all.

Just after you pass the refrigerator, the wall then turned to the right and recessed about four feet back into the kitchen to form a five-foot-wide U-shaped area. On this wall was a chest-high built-into-the-wall split-level gas oven. The oven was encased with cherry oak cabinets that went from the floor to the ceiling. The opposite wall of the U had more cherry oak floor cabinets with the hunter green granite countertop and cherry oak wall cabinets as well. So while you were cooking at the stove top, you could walk right across the kitchen to check on what you were baking in the oven.

I should mention here that I have never actually taken a tap measurer and measured my mother's kitchen. This was a sometimes boring occupational habit of mine. It is easier for me to see in my mind's eye any structure or area when I can place measurements to them. Still—I'm willing to wager a year's worth of my company's earnings that if the measurements of this kitchen were taken—I wouldn't be off by more than a few inches.

On the two recessed walls, the one between the freezer and refrigerator and the one that formed the base of the U where the oven is, the walls were decorated with mosaic tiles that were the same desert sand color as the dinette chairs. These mosaic tiles also formed pictures of tulips in the center of the walls. The stem and leaves of the flowers were made from mosaic tiles that were hunter green in color while the tulips themselves were made from tiles that were either rose color pink or cherry red. The kitchen floor was laid with a rose-pink-colored porcelain tiles that had needle-thin red veins running all throughout them. These tiles made the floor seem luminous and helped to brighten up the kitchen.

Each week, my sister and I had our night to cook dinner. At its widest area, the kitchen measured fourteen feet across, and it was nineteen feet long. Can you imagine how it felt for a kid trying to cook a meal in a kitchen this size? Even though my mother helped out in the beginning, it still took some getting use too. And it certainly didn't help, in the first place, that I didn't like the fact that I had to do this every week. To add insult to injury, we each had weekly chores of keeping this monstrosity of a kitchen clean. We had to wash the dishes each night; fortunately, the dishwasher helped out there. But "one must learn the proper way to load a dishwasher, mustn't one?"

Then there was the floor itself. We had to sweep the kitchen floor using a soft cloth dust mop, and of course, you wouldn't think of walking in the kitchen in your shoes. No, they came off as soon as you walked through the front door. Next, the floor had to be mopped as well. The pink tiles were very pretty to look at, but they were also very easy to get dirty. This meant that the kitchen floor had to be mopped every other night during the jail sentence we had each month. Thankfully, we would get three weeks off because my mother would alternate cleaning the kitchen with us the other two weeks of the month. These times she would clean the kitchen the way it was supposed to be done, as she would say.

My sister, on the other hand, seemed to love cooking and would have gladly done my cooking for me, but my mother wouldn't allow that to happen. So I had to learn how to, a month in advance, decide what meals I wanted to cook, and then determine the ingredients that would be needed to prepare the meals, and then give the list to my mother so the items would be available when I needed them. The thing I think I hated the most about this whole ordeal was the fact that we didn't get to cook on the same night each week.

If I cooked dinner on Monday night one week then the next week I would have to cook dinner on Tuesday night. The week after that, it would be Wednesday. The meal you cooked on a Sunday was quite different from the meal you cooked on a Saturday for example. So we also had to learn how to prepare meals for different occasions. For a young teenage boy, having to cook dinner and clean the kitchen only seemed to frustrate and anger me.

Years later, having the opportunity to reflect back, I finally got it! My mother was instilling in us values such as discipline, work ethics, and responsibilities that would forever shape our adult lives. Today, for example, I run my company using many of the principals I learned from having to cook and clean my mother's kitchen. I have to decide what materials will be needed for jobs that won't start for several months. I have to plan the weekly work schedules for employees on different projects, and I have to keep track of plans, bids, and monthly invoices all while having a family of my own to keep up with. All this comes as second nature to me now, thanks to my mother's influence.

She also made sure to instill these values in us at a very early age. At age twelve, I may no longer have to attend church, but I certainly had to cook dinner and clean the kitchen when my turn came. I don't think—in fact, I'm pretty sure that the idea never occurred to me—that morning my mother came into my room to have our little talk that being mature meant that I would be released from one form of restriction such as attending church, only to be bound again with another form of restriction such as cooking dinner and cleaning the kitchen.

In spite of all the misgivings I had about the kitchen chores my sister and I had to do, once my own kids reached the tender age of twelve, they too had to learn to cook dinner and clean the kitchen. They didn't like it either! They always wondered why it was so funny to me when they got so upset when their turn came to clean the kitchen, but I would be thinking, "What are you getting upset about? You should just be glad you didn't have to clean my mother's kitchen."

Thanks to my mother, I saw the same character instilled into my kids that she made sure to instill in us. They both know the meaning of responsibility and purpose, and they know how to feed themselves, and that's all my mother ever wanted for me and my sister.

CHAPTER 4

A Daughter's Love

So there we were, my sister and me, standing in the foyer of the house that helped to shape us into the people we became. A house which my mother hadn't changed anything from the time we both left home. *My* mother was very particular that way; maybe even a little eccentric in that way, yet it was strangely reassuring to see everything still in their proper place. After my few moments of reflection, I turned my attention back to my sister to see that she, too, had a faraway look on her face. Only she wasn't looking in the direction of the kitchen; she was staring in the direction of my mother's bedroom.

To the right of the foyer was the stairwell that led to the second floor. Just beyond these stairs was the hallway that led to my mother's bedroom, and it was this room that had captivated my sister's attention. By the expression on her face, I could see that it was the painful memory of the loss of my mother that had her firmly within its grasp. Cautiously, I asked, "Is everything okay?"

"I don't know if I can do this" was the whisper that came as her reply.

My sister is very sensitive, and she feels everything very deeply. She once told me that she had to imagine a bright white light surrounding her as a shield to keep out the feelings of everyone she came into contact with, or she would become weak and sick from all the pain she felt from other people's emotions, and that it's only when she was among children that she felt at peace. I just listened.

What can a person say to something like that? I didn't know if this was something she read somewhere and then decided that she had this condition, or if this idea was something she thought up herself. I didn't know!

But it was clear to me, at the time, that she believed every word of what she was saying. So standing there, I knew I had to do something quick to reassure her that everything was going to be okay, or she was going to shatter into a million pieces. She took the death of my mother very hard, and she even wanted to sue the doctors because she felt that the surgery they performed on my mother was supposed to save her life; not to have it end a few short months later.

Nothing prepared me for what my mother's death would do to my sister. The reason it has taken us so long to reach this point of coming back here to move my mother's things out was because of how fragile my sister became after my mother's death. She became a little girl lost without her mommy. The tears never seemed to stop flowing down her face, and she wasn't going in to work which, for her, meant that she had lost her way and was no longer able to be herself because being around her kids has always been the joy of her life. The sad thing was that for a very long time, I wasn't able to be much help to her because of what I was feeling and what I was going through. I felt I was barely able to keep it together myself.

Finally, after allowing her several months of latitude, I decided that I had to do something for both our sakes. Luckily, for her, three of those months she had off from school anyway. But as the new school year was about to begin, I thought it was time to let her know how I was feeling, that I had to let her see that I was hurting too. So one day, I went to see her, and we sat and just cried together! She saw just how much pain I was in! For some reason, when a women see a man cry, it makes her turn from her own sorrow and find compassion for him.

My sister, for the first time in her life, had to comfort me that day. That simple act of sharing with her the pain I was going through was what pulled her out of the depths of despair. And now, standing there, I could see that unless I did something, she would be slipping away again. So I put my arm around her shoulders, and I told her that we still had each other. I told her that I wasn't going anywhere, and that I would always be there for her. No matter what, she will always be able to count on me. I also told her that I could feel Mom's presence at times. That I knew she was still watching over us, and then I turned and yelled out into the house, "Willa, I know you're watching over us!"

These words seemed to help bring her back to me, and I could see the light returning into her eyes. Not that she necessarily believed me because I have always teased her about her beliefs. But I think it was more because she saw how concerned I was for her—a concern that I've had to, as her brother, show her many times in our lives. She knew that if I was willing to call on the supernatural, then I was really worried about her.

As her big brother, as she always calls me, I knew exactly what I was to do and exactly what I was to say in that situation from a lifetime of looking after my sister. From a lifetime of encouraging her and a lifetime of protecting her—sometimes from herself. A lifetime of being there for her after one failed relationship after another. Once again, this was a time that she needed me to tame the rage that existed just beneath the surface of her pleasant personality, to calm the turbulent sea of her mind, and to still the restlessness of her soul. So I told her that we didn't even have to go into that room today. We could just leave it for another day, another time, and just take care of clearing out our rooms upstairs. She finally smiled, and then I knew everything was going to be okay.

CHAPTER 5

A Very Unusual Art Gallery

After we each had, for different reasons, our moments of painful reflections, and had enough time to sufficiently recover from them, we embark on the stairs that you must first walk up facing toward the front of the house until you reach the first landing, and then turn back toward the interior of the house to continue up the stairs to the second floor where our bedrooms were. Once you reach the top of the stairs, the stairwell let out into a viewing and sitting platform area that was—including the four feet for the width of the hallway—about eleven feet in depth.

The platform was protected around its outer edge by a black cast-iron railing that prevents you from falling over the edge. The opening into the viewing area of the platform was also the same seven feet in width as the foyer downstairs. The measurement from the end of the foyer, which was the beginning of the living room, to the back of the living room was approximately twenty-nine feet. So standing at the railing on the second floor afforded you a twenty-two-foot downward view of the living room and dining room. The dining room was only used on special occasions and when family would stay over during the holidays.

Standing at the railing of the viewing gallery, which was what my mother use to call this area, you were immediately confronted with a spectacular panoramic view of the mountainous wooded area directly behind the house. The hill side sloped down until it reached the wide expanse of the Potomac River in the center of its valley. On this level of the house, the entire exterior wall—as also was the case for the wall behind the white drapes in the living room and dining room downstairs—of the back of the house was made of huge glass-pane windows that seem to individually capture picturesque scenes of the landscape outside. To stand there at this railing during the course of a year looking through the glass windows made you feel as if you were standing in some very unusual art gallery where the paintings on the walls changed with the changing of the seasons.

The view these imaginary paintings displayed through the glass-pane windows of the back of the house was nothing short of one being given a special privilege to see the miraculous stages of nature in action. The imaginary paintings of the spring months were the most spectacular and the most succinct evidence of the creative process one could observe. Each morning, on this immense make-believe canvas, a great and wonderful artist would add more beautiful touches to this astonishing ever developing landscape scene he was painting. With the strokes of his magical brush, the brown earth of winter would, just about overnight, turn into a beautiful emerald-green sea of grass and foliage.

One day, there would be nothing but little green shoots forcing their way up through the earth. The next day, these same shoots would start to develop buds on them. Then in a few days, these buds would be exploding into the most amazing array of colors and shades of reds, orange, yellows, greens, blues, indigo, and violets of the most beautiful flowers imaginable. It was almost as if you were watching a marvelous depiction of still life in real life.

The trees that had, during all the months of winter, gone barren would now come to life and start to cover their nudity with leaves as if they were a woman dressing herself in her finest apparel. This artist would find no time to rest his brush but would day after day continue to magically create this imaginary beautiful landscape painting until finally, what you were viewing through the glass-pane windows of my mother's house was indeed, "A masterpiece!"

The summer months were also quite beautiful, but in a different way. The effects the oppressive heat of the summer sun would have on the landscape were also apparent in these imaginary paintings. Although the scenery changed very little during this time, the stress each form of plant life was enduring during the long hot, dry days would be evident in the drooping flowers, the browning grass, the low-hanging branches, and the stillness of the leaves on the trees as if the summer landscape had somehow became a Salvador Dali original.

Until finally, the rain would come and refresh and renew everything back into vibrant colors again. As if nature itself, like a patient lying on an operating table, needed to be resuscitated back life. Repeatedly during the course of the summer months, the rain would revive the landscape by bringing it back to life, and each time, it would appear brand-new again. Anyone who has ever witnessed the effect water has on plant life would certainly attest to the statement that water is the true elixir of life.

The fall months, like the spring, was also an extraordinary exhibition of the magical brush of this artist. Just as the chameleon is ever-changing its color, the leaves of autumn would shift in color as if they, too, had the ability to refract light's rays. They would go from the greenest greens to the faintest yellows, dullest orange, rustic reds, deepest purples, and darkest browns in only a few short weeks.

The view from this area of the house during the autumn's harvesting of the trees, as the leaves began to change colors and fall to the ground, would leave an ever increasing unobstructed line of sight to the Potomac River. As the river flowed through Virginia on its ever-flowing southward course, it was still clean and unpolluted. The water still sparkled in the sunlight and would be so clear; you could see that it was teaming with life just below its surface.

Everywhere else where there was once life abundant was now beginning to fade and die. Whereas the spring season was the bursting forth of new life and vitality. The fall was the gradual decaying and eventual death of that life. It was the exact opposite energy of the spring. It was an awesome display of the wonders of the cycle of life and nature being captured on the canvas of this great artist.

Lifeless, cold, and barren; nevertheless, the paintings of the winter months were of Hallmark quality. Any of these views of the snow-covered trees and the pristine snow-covered landscape, undisturbed by human footprints, would make the perfect seasonal greeting card, and a perfect winter scene painting captured in the glass-pane windows. My mother would often take pictures of these natural winter festivities through the windows of the house, or she would stand on the patio deck to make sure she got as many angles as possible of the beautiful scenery just outside our backdoor. Then she would have them made into Christmas cards and send them out to family and friends. My sister and I used to love to help her pick out the scenery shots we wanted to send to our friends. It was such a wonderful time of the year.

To the left of the viewing gallery opening, on the side with the iron railing, there was a five-foot-wide passageway that continued down the left wall facing the rear of the house for about twelve feet until it reached a black leather cushion sofa with two sterling silver floor lamps on either side of it. As a child, I imagined these lampstands to be two sentries standing there on guard. They stood tall and erect with each having two extending flexible appendages, which could be adjusted to focus their light wherever needed. To me, these appendages looked like the arms of these two witnesses as they witnessed this glorious succession of the rising and setting of the sun on this breathtaking scenery viewed from the back of the house.

On clear nights, they would be at their post to watch the moon pass through its phases from a thin sliver of a crescent shape until it became the symbol for perfection—a perfect full round orb in the night sky. How amazingly beautiful it was to sit on this sofa and watched the moon go through its phases as it became full. The back of the sofa could also lay flat to provide an extra bed when there were several guests staying over.

On the far side of the sofa was a black card table with a sterling silver reading table lamp sitting on it and two black folding chairs on either side. The table provided a surface to hold your material if what you were reading required its use. Most of the time, though, I would just sit and enjoy the view.

CHAPTER 6

The Princess and the Guest Quarters

My sister and I had already agreed beforehand that we would only take our personal things that day and that we would also collect all the personal items we each wanted of our mother's, but in light of the events of the day, I thought it best to put that part of our assignment on hold. The movers would be coming in a few weeks to box up and move all the remaining things, so we still had time to revisit that idea.

The living room furniture was to go to my house, and everything in the kitchen and dining room was going to Rachael's. She also mentioned that she wanted my mother's bedroom furniture as well. Everything else would be placed in storage until we decide if we were going to sell the house or not. So it was only our bedrooms that we had to concern ourselves with that day.

When we were little, this would have meant that once we reached the top of the stairs, we both would have turned right to walk down the hallway to our bedrooms. The first door on the left would be the door to my sister's room, and then the next door would be my room. In between the two rooms on the opposite side of the hallway was the door to the bathroom.

I think it was around that time, maybe as early as twelve, my sister no longer wanted to share the same bathroom, and she began to petition my mother to let her move into the guest bedroom at the other end of the hallway. She felt, as she was starting to get older, she needed to have more privacy. Back then, I didn't really understand what all the fuss was about, so it didn't matter to me one way or the other. My mother did eventually grant my sister her request as long as she understood that when there were out of town guests, she would have to temporally move back into her original bedroom.

The guest bedroom was more like a hotel suite, and we use to jokingly call it "The Guest Quarters." Three feet down the hallway, after you pass the entrance to the viewing gallery, you come face to face with the four-foot-wide door to the guest bedroom. The door was made of solid wood. It was stained with a shiny black lacquer, and it even had a knocker. Both the knocker and the door handle were plated gold. Behind that door was a suite three times the size of my bedroom with a walk-in closet, which was almost the size of my bedroom by itself. The walk-in closet had wall-to-wall carpet unlike my room where the carpet stops at the sliding doors to the closet. It had a marble Jacuzzi tub in the bathroom with matching marble wall and floor tiles.

The marble tile floor extended all the way to the opposite wall of the bedroom directly in front of the bathroom. This area was where my sister created her fairytale fantasy. She had a vanity table with a matching mirror and a matching chair that had a pillow soft cushion seat. The table, mirror, and chair were white with pink trim going along their edge. All the knobs to the drawers were also pink, and the cushion in the chair was also pink. The mirror had those little round light bulbs all along its edge, which lit up from a switch on the wall.

Oh, by the way, my pet name for my sister is Rache, and she would spend hours at that table staring into that mirror. She would change her hair, change her face, and even change her clothes. Her hair had to be just right. Her makeup had to be just right. Her clothes had to match her hair and her makeup. She would try so many different outfits and looks on that my mother would have to decide for her what she was going to wear, and usually only allowed her to wear a plain lipstick.

Although my mother wouldn't allow my sister to paint the walls pink and purple like she wanted to, she did allow her to choose the colors for anything that could be removed from the room. So there were a lot of pink and purple things in her room. And since her room was right above the kitchen, it was basically the same size as the kitchen except it actually extended to the exterior wall of the side of the house, whereas the kitchen had an entrance on its far wall that opened up into the dining room. So this should give you some idea of just how big the guest quarter was, and still my sister managed to completely fill this room with all her stuff.

In my sister's bedroom was the huge closet that I mentioned filled with all the clothes she had from the time she was a little girl all the way up to high school. And shoes! I think she has, in her closet, the first pair of shoes she ever wore and every other pair she wore until she left for college. Proudly displayed on several shelves throughout her room were her very extensive doll collections—from her Barbie doll collection to her American Girl and Heritage doll collections. She probably has every doll ever made for each of her collections. She has stacks and stacks of teen magazines—*Sweet Sixteen*, *Junior Miss*, and countless others dating back several years. Not to mention all the bookshelves filled with all the volumes of books she read on a wide array of all the strange and weird subjects that interest her, and those were just the things I knew about; who knows what else is in that room.

My sister, also, must have been contemplating the task she would have to undertake to clean out her room. She turned to me and said, "If you help me with my room, I will help you with yours."

"Yeah, Rache, I can see why you would want that to happen, but even with both of us trying to put everything you have in that room in boxes, it would still take us the rest of the night and all day tomorrow. You wanted that room ever since you were a little girl. You always wanted to be the princess living in her royal chamber. Well, Your Highness, the royal chamber has to be boxed up and packed away now, and your humble servant won't be able to help you this time," I said.

"You know what, Raphael, I think you missed your calling. You should have been a comedian." Jerk!

"Seriously, sis, it is a very nice room, and you really did a number on mom with all that 'I need my privacy' act. She bought it hook, line, and sinker. But I always knew that it was just the fantasy of living in that room for you."

"You did? Why didn't you say anything to Mom?"

"Well, for one, you and Mom had that female bonding thing going on. That female telepathy thing that all women seem to share. You and Mom understood each other without even having to say much to each other most of the time.

"The other reason was that it made you so happy to be in that room. I couldn't take that away from you. Besides, I think deep down, Mom really knew why you wanted that room. You two just got each other's moods and feelings right all the time. Anyway, it wasn't just that room that you and Mom shared a simpatico understanding. Remember how Mom always told me to sit in the back seat of the car when we went somewhere? If I was to learn to be a gentleman, she would say, then I needed to start while I was young. So you always got to sit in the front seat next to Mom while I sat in the back.

"Everything Mom ever asked us to do, it always seemed so natural for you. You just did everything like it made perfect sense. While for me, I never felt like I understood half of the things Mom made us do. I always felt like I was the odd man out, especially after Dad died. I know now that her telling me to sit in the back seat was helpful for me in developing the proper attitude I should have toward women, but it didn't seem like that back then. It just seemed like you two had a special relationship, and I was just the son who didn't have a dad."

"Obi, Mom loved you so much! You don't think she knew you were growing up without a father? She was always so proud of you. Why do you think she made sure you joined the Boy Scouts? And of course, you excelled at that. You made Eagle Scout in no time at all. When you wanted to learn to play the bass guitar, she made sure you got the one you wanted. And again, without any formal training or even a professional teacher, you learned to play, and even had a band for a while in junior high school.

"I can't even tell you how proud she was that you did that all on your own. She never said anything to me. You are just going to have to believe me. She was very proud of you. And later on, even though you never really needed one because you always got good grades, she made sure you had a tutor. But really, you had two tutors because Nancy introduced you to her boyfriend Tom.

"In the beginning, Nancy was helping both of us with our homework, until she saw that you didn't really need her help, then she would just help me. Maybe she and Mom talked or something because Tom started taking you on camping and fishing trips, and you two developed a bond like he was a substitute father for you.

"I never got to go camping or fishing even though Nancy went on most of the overnight trips with you two. I still couldn't go and I wanted too. But Mom wanted you to have that male bonding experience all for yourself. One day, you picked up a pencil and somehow figured out that you could draw just about anything you looked at. Mom immediately rushed out to get you the art supplies you needed. Had she not done that, do you think you would have been selected to attend art school before you graduated from high school or have the business you have today?

"When you wanted to join our high school football team, even though she was so worried that you might get hurt, Mom sign the permission slip because she wouldn't let her motherly concerns prevent you from developing into the man she knew you would be. And again, you excelled at that sport too, becoming a star player until you got hurt. Do you know when it was the first time I ever saw Mom cry? It was the day you had to be placed in the ambulance. So if I were you, I wouldn't think that Mom and I had such a special relationship. It was a great relationship for a mother and daughter to have, and she loved me without any doubt, but she loved me as a mother loves her daughter. It's a maternal thing that a woman feels for her daughter, but the pride of any woman is her son. She was always very proud of you!"

"Wow! Rache, you're good! You really had me going for a minute too! You're just trying to butter me up so I will help you clean out the guest quarters—right!"

Really, I knew that wasn't what was happening. I just had to change the subject because everything she had just said was true. Rachael saw what I was doing and decided she would play along too.

THE PULL

"Oh, please, Obi! Please! Help your poor little no talent, ungifted sister out. Please, sir, let some of the bread crumbs fall from you table so the poor can share in your great blessings and wealth!"

Was she joking? Yes! Did she just seize the opportunity to throw in a little sarcasm? You betcha!

CHAPTER 7

Sister Witch and Brother Magneto

"Rache, don't forget, I still have to have enough time to check out the attic before we leave here tonight. That is, unless, you plan to go up and help me," I said.

"No! That won't be necessary! I trust a big strong man like you can handle anything you encounter up there. Besides, by now there could be mice or squirrels living up there, or worst still, bats! At any rate, there will definitely be spiders and cobwebs or any number of other types of bugs all over the place up there. I won't be willingly walking into some type of bug hive, colony, or nest tonight, thank you very much!"

In spite of her protest about the possibility of small rodents and bugs living in the attic, the real reason why my sister won't venture into the attic was because there was no way my sister would ever climb up laddered stairs which entered into complete darkness and search for a pull string to turn on the light. So I had already assumed, upon entering the house, that I would be the one to take care of that chore.

"Rache, we both know you don't want to go up there because it's dark and spooky. I know you tried to explain this to me once before, but can you indulge me and explain why someone who believes in all the things you believe in is afraid of the dark? I wouldn't even think that would be possible since you're like a witch or something, right?"

"Don't be juvenile, Raphael. We light workers don't prefer the term witch anymore. That term conjures up an image of a wicked, evil old lady dressed all in black with a big black mole on her face and a black cat at her side," she said.

"But, Rache, don't you have a black cat, and isn't most of the clothes you wear black?"

"Yes! Sheba is black and my wardrobe does tend to consist mostly of black items, but I'm not a wicked, evil old lady with a mole on my face now, am I?"

"Not yet" were the barely audible words of my reply.

"What? What did you say! Did you say something you wanted me to hear, Raphael?" she said.

I thought the best way out of the situation was to use the "hunch your shoulders and look confused" strategy.

"No! I didn't say anything."

"You think you're so funny, don't you?" In spite of her faint attempt at being angry, she couldn't resist smiling when those words left her lips.

"Anyway, I'm not afraid of the dark, not like you and Mom always believed. Ever since I was a little girl, I could feel the energy people left in a place. Most of the time these energies were kind and friendly, but everybody is not always good. Sometimes there's energy left in a place of people who did very bad things in their lives. These energies grow stronger at night and exist in darkness. So most places need to be cleans of the evil spirits before you move into them. I simply prefer not to enter into a dark place without first performing a cleansing ritual, and yes, before you say anything, this ritual is usually performed during the daylight hours."

"Yeah, sis, but how practical is that, really? What about a movie theater? If what you are saying is true, then you would never be able to go see a movie."

"Obi, we light workers know that we can't control every situation in life. Of course, we try to live a normal life as much as possible. So if we have a really bad omen or feel bad vibes about a place or a situation when we want to do normal things like normal people, we believe there's strength in numbers."

"Do you remember the last time I went to see a movie? Yeah, we went to see the Bruce Lee festival at the Arlington Drafthouse when you broke up with that kung fu guy. What was his name?"

"His name was Jeremy!" she said.

"Yeah, that's right—Jeremy! You dragged me to watch those movies with you so you could get over him. You said you wanted to just have a few beers, eat good food, and watch Jeremy get his butt kicked. He became the villain in the movies, and you imagined he was the one Bruce Lee was beating to a pulp. But you told me Jeremy never put his hands on you. Was that true or not?"

"Yes, that's true. Jeremy wouldn't have even dream of hurting me. He just turned out to be a jerk that's all."

"Okay then, what I thought happened must have been true," I said.

"Please, enlighten me, oh, great wise one. What did you think happened?" she asked.

"He probably couldn't handle all your witchie-poo stuff."

"Witchie-poo, that's a good one even for you, Obi! Yeah, maybe it was that, and the fact that he cheated on me!"

"He did, Rache? You should've told me. I'm sorry!"

"Oh, well, that's all in the past now, I have long since gotten over him, and by the way, I have never had to drag you to go see Bruce Lee. You know you love Bruce Lee movies."

"Okay, maybe. But what does that night have to do with what we're talking about now?"

"It was just you and me that night, right?"

"Yeah, I told Birdie that you had just broken up with your boyfriend, and I was going to take you out to dinner and a movie. Okay—so?

"Well, I felt safe to go to the movies with you. Obi, I have always felt safe when I'm with you. You don't know how powerful you are or could be if only you were willing to acknowledge the truth! But to be honest, I think you just refuse to accept that you have this tremendous ability."

"What ability, Rache? You've said this stuff before. I'm really not in the mood for this conversation."

"Obi," my sister's eyes were softening and a motherly concern was now appearing on her face, "do you really think we could be as close as we are, as we have always been, and I am not able to see these things about you? It takes one to know one, Obi. I know that there is some hidden side to you that you refuse to let anyone see. I have seen what electronic devices do when you touch them sometimes. I have seen what happens in times when you let your guard down and are not focusing so hard on appearing normal. I have seen how before you even touch them, they respond to you as if you are already moving their controls.

"I've seen how the TV and the computer screens get blurred when you walk by them. I've seen other strange things about you too! Don't you think, for one minute, that I haven't been watching all these years? You have an energy that radiates from you. I can feel it whenever I'm with you. I have always been able to sense this about you."

"Woo! Woo! That's some very scary stuff you got there, Rache! That's some very powerful evidence you have of my so-called psychic abilities! Don't you know that everything you just described can be attributed to static electricity?"

"Okay, Magneto, you know it's only because of your rigid and stubborn belief system that prevents you from acknowledging these gifts you have. You think that everything in life can be explained in a textbook. But in truth, all that type of reading really does is block the flow of your chi. The real answers to life's major questions can only be found by allowing the free flowing of your charka energies."

"Rache! What in the world are you talking about now?"

"Oh, never mind. You wouldn't understand anyway! Since you seem to think you always have an answer for everything, then riddle me this, Batman! What about those other times we've been together and strange things happened to us?"

I may have neglected to mention that, like me, my sister is a big DC and Marvel comic book fan, and we would, at times, slip in and out of role-playing characters during our conversations, but this time, I didn't think I had ever seen her so serious before. So I wasn't sure if it would have been a good idea for me to play along. She seemed to be so frustrated with me, I was a little afraid for my safety! I thought she might turn me into a toad or something!

CHAPTER 8

An Unidentified Flying Object

"Do you remember that day when we were driving home from school, and we saw that thing in the sky?" Rachael said.

"Okay, here we go again!" I said.

"Yes, Raphael, here we go again! When will you accept the truth about what happen that day? What did you say it was at first?"

"I said it looked like a large sheet of plastic."

"Yeah, that's what you said all right! A perfectly square-shaped sheet of plastic the size of a house just sitting—no, hovering—in the sky, right?"

"Okay, I admitted to you that that didn't make sense, but I'm still not willing to make the leap in logic you made. Just because it's something that I can't explain doesn't mean that I'm supposed to automatically assume it came from another planet, Rache!"

"How can you even say that, Raphael, when we both saw this thing that was first hovering just above the house tops and slowly start to rise in the sky? Then once it was about the height of the clouds, it changed from being transparent into the shape of a disc and sped away."

"Rache, it was more like a top shape not a disc shape."

"At first, Raphael, it looked like a top, but then it changed into a disc just before it flew away."

"If you say so, by then it was so high up in the sky, it wasn't much bigger than a dot. So if you say it changed into a disc, then it changed into a disc."

"Raphael, I will never understand how you can refuse to accept something so obvious! Dude, you're in denial! That was probably one of the most amazing experiences a person can have in this lifetime, and you treated it like it was just another ordinary event in your life. It perplexes me how you can stand here, even after all this time, and not see how unique and singular that entire situation was."

"Obi," now her eyes were almost pleading with me to accept her conclusion, "it was a once in a lifetime occurrence, and it should have been a life-altering experience for not just me but you as well."

"That night when I told Mom what happened—"

"Wait! You told Mom?"

"Yes, of course, I told Mom! You mean to tell me you didn't?"

"No, Rache, I didn't tell Mom. I didn't tell anyone."

"Raphael, how could you keep something like that to yourself? Who are you? What are you? Are you even human! What have you done to my brother!" She said all that while shaking her head as if she was both dismayed and disgusted with me at the same time.

"Anyhow, I told Mom that for some reason I wasn't frighten because I knew that I was with you. Somehow, I knew that everything was going to be okay because you were there—because we were together! Have you ever given any consideration to that fact? We were together when we saw that thing! That, by itself, should mean something to you. It should. Why? If you could ever get anything through that thick skull of yours, it should mean that we were chosen to witness that together," she said.

I couldn't tell my sister that I saw that same object in the sky the day before while I was standing in the front yard. I saw that same sheet of plastic in the sky. But only this time it appeared to be waving back and forth as if it was being blown by a strong wind across the sky. When I noticed that there was no wind that day, I had to assume that there must have been a high current of wind up there blowing this huge piece of plastic. That explanation, I forced myself to accept, only caused me to be gripped with a sudden fear that made me hurry into the house.

I managed to pick back up with my sister's conversation without her even noticing that I had drifted away for a few moments. "Then I told Mom that we weren't the only ones to see it. I explained to her that as the thing began to move, we followed it in the car until we ended up on a dead-end wooded street. And that we thought we were the only ones back there until we noticed another car had also followed the object. Once the disc flew away, we drove right past the other car, and we saw that it was a woman sitting in the driver's seat staring up into the sky where the object had just been."

"Rache, have you ever wondered why that woman, who appeared to be Hispanic and in her late thirties to early forties, kept looking up into the sky as we drove by? That thing in the sky had already left, but she just kept staring up into the sky. Don't you think that if she was really back there to observe that object, she would have wanted to see the expressions on our faces just to confirm that we saw what she thought she just saw? Instead, she never made eye contact with us."

"You do realize, don't you, that we never actually saw her whole face? That's what I thought was so strange about that day! She acted like she was back there to observe us not the object. Wait! Let me get this straight: Out of everything we saw that day, from a large sheet of plastic hanging in midair to a flying disc, you thought the lady sitting in her car was the strangest thing you saw, Raphael? Really!

"Well, that's very funny to me because you said you never told Mom anything about that day, right? Yeah, that's right, why? Because when I told Mom about the lady sitting in the car, she had the same reaction you had. She was more interested in her than she was in the UFO we had just seen."

"Again, Rache, I will only agree to the use of that terminology if you are using it in its literal sense. It was an unidentifiable flying object. But if you are going to insist on identifying it as a spaceship from another planet, then that's where the discussion changes for us."

"Dude, lighten up! If you want to play Doctor Paranoid, then I'll pretend I'm your patient and I'll go along with you, okay!"

"All I'm saying is that Mom started asking some of the same questions you asked about her. She wanted to know if the lady said anything to us. Did she look strange in anyway? Did she pay any attention to you in particular? Why would she ask that, Obi? Why would mom be worried about a strange lady paying special attention to you?"

"I don't have any idea, Rache!"

"You don't, really, Raphael! You don't have any clue why Mom would be thinking that someone was watching you, and yet you just said you thought the woman was back there watching us too! Mom wouldn't explain why she felt that way, and of course, you never explain anything to anybody at any time. But that's not exactly true, is it? She paused as if she was waiting for a response from me, but I had none. At any rate, after Mom saw that I couldn't provide her with the answers to her questions, for some inexplicable reason, she changed the subject and started talking about you and Birdie and her and dad. She started describing to me how it felt the first time she met Dad. She said, 'Rachael, the first time I saw your father, it was like our entire bodies became giant magnets and we were being pulled toward each other against our own will!' That's what she called it, Obi. She called it 'the pull!'

"She actually said the pull was so strong that she instantly knew that she would die if she didn't have Dad. She said she had never experienced anything like it in her entire life. She also said that she knew the moment you met Birdie that you, too, had experienced this pull. What kind of crazy talk is that, Obi? How can someone know just by looking at a complete stranger that they would be willing to die if they don't have that person in their life? I mean, I have seen some guys that I thought were very handsome and all, but I have never felt that I would die right then and there if I never saw them again. That's absurd—right!

"Do you think this pull thing is the reason why Mom never remarried after Dad died? She never even dated another man, and Mom could've had any man she wanted. Raphael, can you please tell me what type of twisted logic was Mom using to put a lady sitting in a car supposedly watching you, even though I'm in the car with you, and the day you met you wife together! And what did she mean when she said she knew you experienced this pull also? Just tell me what she was talking about, Raphael! For once in your life, just tell me the truth—tell me!"

"Calm down, Rache, I don't have any idea why mom thought those two events related to each other—honest! Look, I know you think I'm this secretive person hiding all these deep dark mysteries from you, but I just think that we are different. You're this open and honest person who isn't afraid to show her feelings and emotions. You, at once, like everybody you meet. You believe in everybody you meet, and even though it unusually doesn't turn out too well for you. You trust everybody you meet. You don't seem to ever consider the danger of any situation.

"Where most people experience a feeling of caution and apprehension about a person, you usually only see novelty and excitement in those situations. Sometimes, I marvel at how easily it is for you to just accept things at face value. I'm amazed at how uncomfortable you are when you are among a crowd of people, yet anyone from that crowd can walk up to you and immediately be accepted into your life. I admire that quality in you, Rache. The world would be a better place if there were more people like you! But we don't live in a world where people are, for the most part, innocent and naïve. That world, if it even ever existed, is long gone.

"So for me, I tend to distrust everyone's motives initially. Living in the world we live in today, you almost have to be that way. I'm more comfortable when I'm in a crowd because usually, there's no one targeting you with a hidden agenda. I'm more of a 'you have to earn my trust' type of person."

"So, Raphael, you know what you're really saying? You're saying that you don't trust me!"

"Sometimes, Rache, believe it or not, it's best not to know everything. Sometimes the best thing one person can do for another person is to keep them from harm. If one person feels that something may be harmful if they share it with another person, then it becomes the duty of that person to protect the other person from the possibility of getting hurt."

"Unless, Obi, that person also cares about the person that's trying to protect them. Then the person not telling the other person is only causing her to worry about him."

"Rache, I was speaking hypothetically."

"Yeah, Raphael, of course you were."

Sometimes, it's so difficult to be around my sister because she always puts me in the awkward position of having to not be completely honest with her. She, somehow, has the ability to see right through all my defenses. Except for Birdie, whom I'm completely unable to keep a secret from for very long, Rachael is the only other person who intuitively suspects something when I'm not being honest. But this time, I really didn't know what my mother meant by the things she said. It's true though, what she said about Birdie and me. The first time I saw my wife, it was as if every single cell in my body ignited and burst into flames!

The attraction (what my mother apparently called "the pull") I felt for her didn't seem to be originating from within my body. It felt as if it didn't even exist inside my body, but it was coming from someplace outside of me as if it had self-existence on its own and was using my body as a vessel. It was an extremely overpowering sensation, and I could not resist its pull! The next thing I remembered, I was waking up in the hospital. But to tell my sister all this didn't seem to be the right thing to do at that time because the more she recalled the conversation she had with my mother, the more she became upset. She was starting to act as if she felt Mom and I had some secret that she had been excluded from. Truthfully, I didn't even know that my mother understood what happened to me that day I saw Birdie for the first time!

"Oh, wow, Rache," now I was just trying desperately to change the subject, "look at the time! We've been standing here in this hallway talking the whole time, and we haven't even done anything we came here to do. Now it's too late for me to do both my room and the attic. Can you please go get started on your room, and I'll just go take a look up in the attic? Then I'll come back and help you with your room. I guess you're happy now, huh? Your plan worked after all, Your Highness!"

CHAPTER 9

The Attic and the Shoebox

So just as I suspected, it felled to me to be the one to go up and check on what needed to be clean out of the attic. In the hallway that led to my bedroom, on the ceiling just as you reach what used to be my sister's bedroom was the pull string that lets down the stairs that take you up into the darkness that is the attic.

This was another off-limits place for my sister and me when we were growing up. We were never allowed to go into the attic, but I don't think we would have wanted to anyway: It's not the most inviting place to visit. I always thought my mother was afraid that one of us would get hurt, and that's why she forbade us from ever going up there. Once I was up in the attic, I had to walk a few feet until I felt the draw string to turn on the light. Phew, well at least one of my sister's predictions came true. I walked, face first, right into a cobweb.

This first light bulb cast just enough light to illuminate where the string was to the light in the center of the attic. The heat from the sun of the day made the temperature in the attic a few degrees higher than the rest of the house. Not excessively hot but just enough to be uncomfortable. There was no need, any longer, to use the air-conditioner since no one was living here anymore. I'm not sure that it would have made much of a difference, but it may have helped to circulate the air up here. The air was stuffy and smelled stale.

There were particles of dust floating in the air, and everything was also covered in a thin layer of dust. Sheets of plywood had been loosely laid down to cover the exposed floor joists. Between the cracks

THE PULL

created by the wood not being laid down properly, you could see the fiberglass weather insulation that had been rolled down between the joists. Everything in the attic rested on these sheets of plywood, so when you walked, you had to be careful not to miss the plywood and end up with your foot stuck in one of the cracks.

After I managed to get the place well lit, I found myself unintentionally searching for bats. Mice, I thought I could handle, even squirrels wouldn't have been a problem. But bats flying around your head with that screechy noise they make would have been too much to deal with, especially after my sister put the thought in my head. The attic, however, appeared to be free of rodents, flying or otherwise. This assurance allowed me to refocus on my mission.

After giving the attic a precursory overview, there didn't seem to be much that needed to be done. There wasn't much furniture to speak of, only some old folding beach chairs, two folding tables, and two beach umbrellas. There were also some boxes that had the different holiday paraphernalia: boxes for Easter, Halloween, Thanksgiving, Christmas, and of course, the box with the artificial Christmas tree that we had used each year since I was old enough to put that thing together by myself. Once Dad wasn't going to be around anymore to buy a real tree for Christmas, Mom only wanted to use this artificial thing.

On closer examination of the attic, there was an unusual placement of two of the items. Almost directly in the center of the attic under the only other light in the room were two trunks stack on top of each other. This very noticeable placement of the trunks wasn't what made this such an odd and peculiar exhibition, for it was obvious they were placed in that manner to make sure they would be seen.

Each trunk was almost completely covered with the many different stickers of all the places my parents traveled during my father's military days. And I assumed at least one was filled with my father's Navy uniforms, his medals, and badges of honor he received for his tour of duty. The American flag my mother received at his funeral would also be among those things. The other trunk probably contained my mother's wedding dress and all her wedding souvenirs.

Strange, I couldn't recall ever seeing these two trunks before. But stranger still was the fact that sitting on top of them was a large shoebox labeled, "For Raphael."

My first thought was "Oh, no! Legal papers that I was going to have to go through and make sure all my mother's affairs were in order." Why I had that thought I'm not sure because my mother had already taken care of all her financial matters. As with everything she did, all her papers were in perfect order, and her lawyer had handled all her finale arrangements. Maybe it was the fear of the uncertainty of what lay beneath the lid of that box that caused my mind to invent this scenario of paperwork. I'm not sure. Now all I can do is speculate!

I opened the box, however, to find that it was not filled with papers, but instead it contained two stacks of letters. Each stack was tied with a ribbon. One stack had a green ribbon and my grandmother's name was written on a piece of paper under this ribbon that held them together, and the other stack had a yellow-color ribbon with my mother's name written in the same fashion. It is amazing to me how much value women put on certain things. Each stack of letters must have been the size of two yellow pages phonebooks stacked on top of each other. There had to be at least forty to fifty letters in each stack.

My grandmother and mother must have saved every single letter they ever received from my grandfather and father. There were also some very old pictures accompanying them. I thought this whole thing to be very odd, and I didn't know what to make of this discovery. It wasn't until I noticed that there was a folded piece of paper that had, somehow, slipped down along the side of the box that I began to receive any clarity at all. It was a note in my mother's handwriting, and it was addressed to me.

"Raphael, my beloved son," the note began, "when you were still so very young, I tried to prepare you for the coming of the stranger, but I failed. Please forgive me!"

Have you ever been caught so completely off guard that all your mental faculties momentarily freeze causing you to lose track of time, then to suddenly realize that you haven't even moved so much as a muscle for several minutes? This was what happened when I looked down and saw the word *stranger* in my mother's handwriting. I never told my mother anything about my dreams; so for her to now mention a stranger was a complete and total shock to my sensibilities. It left me dazed and confused, and I was baffled as to how on earth could she have known.

"I hope these letters," she continued, "will now help you as my mother's letters helped me. I have arranged them in such a way that they will tell you all that I know about what you are going through. My son, read the letters my mother wrote to me first before she left us. Then read the letters she and my father wrote to each other. Oh, so some of these letters are correspondence they had between each other. That explains why the stacks are so big. Once you've done that, read my letters I wrote to you. It is my last gift to you, my love! Then read the letters your father and I wrote to one another. My darling son, I hope I'm not too late to save you! Love, Mom!"

Save *me*! What did she mean by that statement? How could she have known that my very soul itself would be crying out for deliverance! Glancing over the envelopes, they all seem to have been the love letters of my grandmother and mother. They seem to be the type of thing a mother would leave to her daughter, if to anyone at all. But I was certain that my mother didn't want my sister to read them. She left them in the one place in the house where they could be out in the open, yet my sister would never find them. My mother knew how terribly afraid my sister was of the dark, which meant she wanted only me to find them. So I placed the letters back in their box, closed the lid, sat the box back on the trunks, and turned off the lights.

When I got down from the attic, I went to help my sister with her room.

"Well, how bad is it up there, Obi?"

"I think I'm going to have to come back another day with some help to move the things out of the attic," I replied.

This announcement pleased my sister very much because it was now dark outside, and she didn't like driving at night.

"Yeah, there's not much more I'm going to be able to get done in here tonight either. Why don't we just call it a day? I mean, really, the day wasn't a total waste. We got to spend some time together and talked about things we haven't talked about in years. I think, in that respect, Obi, it was a very productive day."

"All right, Rache, if you think that's best."

"I do! So let me finish with putting these shoes away, and then we can leave."

Secretively, I was also very pleased that we would be leaving because I needed some time to process what I had just discovered.

Once my sister locked the house back up, I had to make sure I could get back in the house without her accompanying me. "Rache, why don't you let me hold the keys this time because chances are I will be able to get a couple of my employees to come back here and help me with the attic before you will be able to get away again from your class?"

"You know, Raphael, you probably still have your own set of keys somewhere in your house. All you would have to do is take the time to look for them."

"You're probably right, but I don't think you realize how many set of keys I have to keep up with already. I have the keys to my house, keys to my office, keys to the warehouse, keys to the company van, and keys to the family cars to worry about. If mom's keys are still in my house, which I'm sure they are, I wouldn't even know where to begin to start looking for them. Look, Rache, I promise I will get another set of keys made and return yours back to you soon."

"Okay, but only if you promise," she stated this as she held the keys dangling from between her fingertips as if they were being offers as a reward to a small child for his obedience.

"I promise!"

After giving my sister a big hug and telling her to drive home safely, I was left standing there alone in my mother's driveway feeling more confused than ever. For reasons I couldn't explain, but for the first time, I was no longer just worried about my own safety. I worried for the safety of my wife, my kids, and now my sister too. Protecting them was now paramount in my life's mission. That's why, although I have consented to tell this story, I have deliberately withheld any description of myself, my sister, and my family that could be used to identify us, and I will continue to do that until I'm giving some type of assurance that those I love will be protected and shielded against any harm that the telling of this story may bring. Unless, I'm forced to reveal their identity against my will, I will not expose my family to the scrutiny the revelation of this information is going to bring.

While driving home, all I could think about was that one time my mother and I had our conversation. Finding that shoebox was like finding a portal to travel back in time! It was a bridge between the past and the present. It felt like that distinct moment in time that you hear about. The moment in a person's life when they know things will never go back to being the way they were before. I knew that if I carried out my mother's instructions concerning those letters, I would never be the same again! I also knew that this was, somehow, all a part of the scheme, of the grand design they have for me in the telling of their story. And now I understood that my mother was a vital component to the revelation I was to make. My mother may have failed to get my attention that day we talked, but she now had my complete and undivided attention!

It was an epiphany!

CHAPTER 10

The College Student and the Professor

When I finally got home that night, the kids were already in bed. I opened the door from the garage that lets into the kitchen, and there was Birdie sitting at the kitchen table. I decided to keep the discovery of the shoebox a secret even from her. I glanced over to look at the clock in the kitchen, and the time was exactly 11:11 p.m. Actually, what I was looking at was the microwave oven, but since Birdie absolutely refuse to cook using a microwave oven, the only purpose ours served was as a kitchen clock.

I said, "Oh, hey, I wasn't expecting you to still be up." My heart was already starting to race in my chest just from the sight of her sitting there! Over the years, I've learned to control what happens to me when I see her, but it is still not without difficulty. I noticed that she didn't respond to my very informal greeting. "You seem to be troubled. Is something wrong? It can wait. First, tell me how did things go at your mother's?"

"Well, you know how it is whenever you plan to do something with Rachael. It's always a small miracle if anything gets done at all. We ended up, or should I say she ended up, talking most of the day away."

"I think it's good, Obi, that you and your sister are so close. I never get the opportunity to see or spend much time with my brothers or my sister because they all live so far away. You should cherish the times you two get to spend together."

"Yeah, I know, and she knows that I love her, but I still have to go back to my mother's to do what we were supposed to do today."

It just seemed convenient, at the time, to blame my sister for my needing to return to my mother's house so soon. Anyway, it was kind of her fault. "I think I'm going to have to go back there early in the morning, and it may take a couple of days to sort everything out, if that's going to be okay with you?"

"Well, it's taken you two a long time to get over the grieving process of the loss of your mother, so however long it takes to be completely healed, I'm willing to wait. I don't know what I would do if something happened to my mother or my father! I just know that I'm not ready to even think about that now. So don't be too hard on your sister. It was her mother that she lost. A girl's mother is very important in her life. You know what, baby, I knew there was a reason why I love you so much!" She smiled.

"Oh yeah, while we're on the subject of my mother's house, I've been thinking about what to do with it. Her house is already paid for, you know that, right?"

"Yes, you told me."

"So I was thinking, we could sell this house and live in my mother's house."

"Honey, your mother's house is twice the size of this house. The kitchen alone would take up almost the entire first floor of our house. Baby, don't you think that may be just a little bit of an exaggeration? Whether it is or not, we really don't need a house that big. What are we going to do with all that space once the kids go off to college? More importantly, who's going to clean a house that size? You're already gone most of the day, and I finally have enough patients to keep me pretty busy during the day also."

"Well, maybe Rache will be willing to move back into her old room. She always seemed to love cleaning everything just like my mother use to do."

"Are you sure she didn't have to clean everything up because your mother told her to do it?"

"I don't know. I know she never complained like I did about having to do it."

"Obi, there's a big difference between doing something because you enjoy doing it and doing it because you're supposed to do it. So unless she actually told you that she enjoyed the responsibility of cleaning your mother's house, which somehow I seriously doubt, you shouldn't automatically assume she did."

"Well, I'm only bringing this up because my mother left the house to both Rachael and me, and neither one of us can sell the house without the other's permission. I can tell you now, if Rachael's reaction today was any indication of what her desire is for that house, then she is not going to be willing to sell it anytime in the foreseeable future. So I'm just saying, I think we should give it a little more thought, or otherwise we may have a house just sitting there that we could live in debt free, while we are living in debt in this house."

"Well, have you talked to your sister about your idea?"

"No, I thought I should run it by you first. You know, honey, I knew there was a reason why I love you so much!" This time, I smiled!

"Now, baby, do you think you can tell me why you are sitting up in the kitchen this time of night looking all sexy and angry!"

"Sexy! Obi, no one was trying to look sexy."

"Oh well, that's a matter of opinion, but you are angry though, right?"

"Well, I wouldn't even call it angry. I just think you need to have a talk with that son of yours."

"What's so funny?"

"Nothing, I just thought I had forgotten your birthday or something. You know, sometimes, you can be so silly, Obi!" She was now laughing, so I knew whatever my son did, it couldn't have been too serious.

"So are you going to tell me what the fruit of my loins has done to cause his very beautiful mother to be 'not really angry with him?'"

"Okay, that boy is going around leaving the toilet seat up in every bathroom in the house, and even then, he's not taking the time to make sure he aims correctly. It's very disturbing to have to touch toilet seats that are covered with yellow stains. So can you talk to him? He's really getting to be too old to still be this inconsiderate of his sister and me."

"Yes, my love! Your wish is my command! Should I tar and feather him first, or do you think a very stern lecture on the subject of the difference between the male and female anatomy will do?"

"Obi, just talk to him, please. Silly man!"

It's always good to make Birdie laugh. You reap great benefits from keeping a smile on her face. But tonight, it was also helping me to calm down and deflate a little from all the pressure I was feeling about the finding I had in my mother's attic. So since this joking around about the situation with my son seem to be lightening up the mood and making both of us feel a little better, I thought I should go with it and have a little fun.

"You know, young lady, there is a scientific explanation for the condition your son is experiencing at this time."

"Oh really, Professor? Could you please elaborate?" Birdie automatically understood what I was doing, and she didn't even miss a beat but jumped right into character. We have always understood each other this way.

"Yes, of course. But perhaps you should get a pencil and a piece of paper so you can take notes?"

"Oh no, professor, I don't think that will be necessary. Someone might actually read these great words of wisdom, and they might become too enlighten!"

"Yes, yes, I see your point. Very well then, only with you will I share my insight, which has come to me after many years of careful research and observation. I'm so eager to hear your take on this subject. I'm all ears, Professor!"

"As you should be because I believe Sigmund Freud and Carl Young themselves would be please with my deduction of the psychological need the male species has to leave the toilet seat up! I think the females of the species have overlooked a vital key in helping them to determine the reason behind the male's compulsion to leave the toilet seat in the up position!"

"Oh, Professor!"

"Not yet, my little college girl—I mean college student! The question they should be asking is not, 'How come he always leaves the toilet seat up?' but rather, 'Why doesn't he ever get upset because the toilet seat is always down?'"

"Oh, Professor, you're so authoritative! The male of the species never complains when he walks into a bathroom and find the toilet seat down. For him, the very act itself, of the lifting up of the toilet seat, resonates deep within his subconscious! Oh, Professor, please, the bell is about to ring!"

"Yes, I'm aware of that fact! So in conclusion, the imagery of the male taking his hand and raising up the toilet seat where he then finds relief is so powerfully imprinted on his subconscious mind that it speaks volumes as to why once he's finish. He leaves the seat in the up position. For him to then lower the toilet seat back down goes against his natural instincts to demonstrate his conquest!"

"Oh, Professor, you're so smart!"

"Yes, my favorite little college student, I think you deserve an A for that very astute observation. Now where did I leave my notebook? Oh yeah, that's right! I believe I left it in the bedroom. Follow me please!"

"Yes, Professor!"

It's now two in the morning, and the euphoria was just starting to fade. Birdie was already fast asleep. Even still, just lying in bed next to her, just being this close to her, gave my body such a feeling of tranquility that the only word I can think of that even comes close to describing this sensation is bliss! Whenever our bodies are separated from each other, a pain begins to grow inside of me. If I'm away from her for more than twenty-four hours, my body actually starts to experience physical pain that gradually becomes so severe that it's almost debilitating. The pull (craving) inside of me for our two bodies to reunite becomes so strong that it becomes unbearable!

So when we are together, there is a feeling of such harmony and peace that it's felt all the way down on the cellular level. This thing, this essence or whatever it is, activates energies inside our bodies that allow us to sense and feel each other's thoughts. But how could I explain something like that to Rachael? How could you explain this

THE PULL

to anyone who hasn't experienced it first hand? And believe me, I've tried. All I got was laughed at and called crazy. Therapy recommendations were also suggested, and my friends started to avoid me.

But tonight, I found out that my mother knew about this thing she called the pull. She also knew about the stranger of my dreams. I got hit with two of the most amazingly shocking revelations all in one night. Now I'm left with trying to figure out what it all means. Now I'm having a hard time trying to fall asleep. In fact, it's starting to appear to me that sleep will not be paying me a visit tonight. I can't stop thinking about that note my mother left me—how desperate her words sounded. I wonder how she could have known about my dreams. Did the same dreams plague her life too? Did she actually meet them?

I understood from the very beginning that I had a role to play in this story of theirs, but now it's becoming increasingly apparent to me that my family's history was also, somehow, very significant to them. I knew that my confrontation would be coming soon, but for now, I was being allowed to find out this information about my family on my own. So for a while, at least or so it would seem, I was only being watched! I don't know how much time I have, but I know I want to unravel this mystery as quickly as possible.

My mother mentioned, in her note, that my grandmother's letters helped her; so that must mean, if I'm correct in my assumption, this nightmare goes back at least as far as my grandmother. Then there were those pictures. I could clearly recognize my mother and father in some of the pictures. My mother and father always contrasted each other so perfectly. My mother being almost charcoal black, and my father always appearing in photographs to be so completely white.

That was the easy part because those were the only pictures in color. The other pictures, however, were very old and in black and white. They were barely in focus, and they had lines running through them like the photographs were starting to turn into jigsaw puzzles. I'm pretty sure, though, that the lady with the long hair was my grandmother, and the tall man standing next to her was my grandfather. As it was the case for the colored pictures, there were other people in the black and white photographs that I just didn't recognized.

They were either standing just off to the side or at times right next to the people in the pictures that I did recognize. These strangers always seemed to be observing what was happening, yet they didn't seem to be notice by the people they were standing right next too. My mother must have felt that those pictures would help to explain the letters to me, or that the letters would help to explain the strangers in the pictures. I wasn't sure which. The only thing I knew for certain was that I had to get back up into that attic to retrieve that shoebox.

CHAPTER 11

Remembering My Mother and My Father

The next morning, the sun's rays had barely broken the horizon before I was up, showered, shaved, dressed, and planning to walk out the door. I was hoping to be gone without having to even wake Birdie or see the kids, but of course, Birdie had other ideas. Just as I was about to give her a goodbye kiss, she opened her eyes and turned to face me.

"Obi, what are you not telling me?"

"Oh, I thought you were still asleep!"

"I haven't really been asleep all night, at least not a sound comfortable sleep. I could feel that something was troubling you during the night, and this kept disturbing my sleep. So what's going on, Obi? Is it the dreams again?"

"Baby, I didn't want to bother you with any of this."

"Honey, it bothers me when you don't talk to me about what you're going through."

Because of this connection Birdie and I share, it does no good for either one of us to try to lie to the other. So I've had to learn that as long as I'm willing to express my honest feelings to Birdie. She will usually be content with knowing that I'm being truthful with her about what I'm willing to share. This method, however, only provides me with a few more additional days. Then I will have to explain everything to her or face the consequences of what trying to avoid the issue will bring. Now though, the trick will be trying to say just enough to assuage her concerns without saying so much as to put her at risk.

"I think my mother and father may have experienced the same type of relationship we have."

"Oh, really, what makes you say that? When I was up in her attic, I found some of their old love letters. I read over one she wrote, and boy, was their some very personal things in that note. It felt like an invasion of privacy. I was a little embarrassed about what I read, and I'm not sure yet what to make of what I discovered up there." Well, I did read over the note my mother left for me, and it did feel like an invasion of my privacy when she spoke of the stranger in my dreams. So I wasn't really lying.

"Honey, it's natural for a child not to see their parents as sexual beings. I'm sure whatever is in those letters are just normal expressions of love a man and a woman felt for each other. For you to be confronted, in that way, with the realization that your parents, at some time in their lives actually, perhaps graphically, expressed their love for each other was probably somewhat of a shock to your system. I think that's a perfectly normal reaction."

"Well, maybe you're right. It was a little disturbing though, to say the least!"

"Honey it must have been a lot disturbing because I don't think you got much sleep at all last night. Are you sure it was just those letters, and this has nothing to do with the dreams?"

"Well, baby, you know that just about everything has something to do with the dreams. I'm just not always sure how or why!"

"Well, you promise when you figure it out, you'll let me know?"

"You know I will!"

"Okay then, you had better get going before it gets late. Oh, don't forget, you have to come home early enough to have your little talk tonight."

"I won't forget, and I will make sure to pick up some tar and feathers just in case their needed."

Taking those few minutes to talk to Birdie didn't cost me as much time as I thought it would. It was still so early; the sun wasn't completely above the horizon yet. So I thought I would turn the radio on to help pass the time as I drove to my mother's. The song that just happened to be playing was Bob Marley's "Rainbow Country" and immediately following that one was another of his songs, "The Sun Is Shining" from his Natural Mystic album.

Oh, I forgot, my kids would tell me I'm supposed to remember to say his Natural Mystic CD. It doesn't do any good to tell them that when these songs were first recorded; they were recorded on LPs, and these vinyl records were called albums and that the word *rainbow* was not associated with the terminology, which it is today, because they will just laugh and call me old.

Anyway, whichever was the correct term to use, album or CD, the songs were very fitting for my early morning drive since the sun was just beginning to shine brightly in the early morning sky. The calming and relaxing affect the songs had on me aided in my decision to take the scenic route to my mother's. By taking the Fairfax County Parkway instead of driving around the Beltway, I managed to avoid most of the rush hour traffic since I was driving in the opposite direction, and I got to enjoy the soothing effect nature had on you when you're driving alone in your car. Only it was my company's van I was driving.

The plan was to make it down to Arlington by noon so I could check on the progress of the work my company was schedule to do at the Carlyle Tower One. This was a very large project, and it was the first big break for my company. We had just won the contract to install all the vinyl, ceramic, and marble tiles in all the units of this new high-rise apartment building. We were to follow the drywall contractor after his men finish their installation. Then the project manager would inspect their work and then give us the okay to start installing in the units once their work was approved.

That's what the meeting was for today—to get the work schedule for the different trades. My foreman, Mr. Whitehorse, was already on the jobsite and would be attending the meeting as well. After this meeting, I was to be home in time for dinner and then have a talk with my son afterward. It wasn't until I reached the exit to get onto Route 7 that I encountered any real traffic concerns. That's when I had no choice but to be in rush hour traffic for a while until I reached the exit that would take me to Great Falls.

Except for that little time I spent on Leesburg Pike, I found most of the drive to be very relaxing, and it gave me a little time to think about something my sister had said the day before. She said I was in denial about what we saw in the sky that day. I didn't think that to be true. If anything, I'm the one who has taken a realistic view of that event. Of course, I have somewhat of an advantage over her. I already know that there are things that can't be explained all alone by our present understanding of science and technology. Whereas she is only guessing, and maybe even hoping; I have experienced it firsthand.

I can tell you that what I experienced didn't appear, to me, to be aliens from another planet. At least they didn't look like aliens. They looked just like you and me. In other words, they looked human! And that's why I'm not buying into the idea that that thing we saw in the sky was from another planet like she keeps going on about. Especially now that my mother has given me hope. Hope that I may finally be able to understand, once and for all, what the hell is really going on in my life.

There are no words that can adequately describe what I'm feeling right now. I'm filled with such anticipation and anxiety over what my mother has to tell me in those letters that I can barely contain my emotions. I have to know what it is she wanted to tell me about the stranger! I have to know how she even knew about my dreams, and how did she know about what happened to me when I first saw Birdie. I'm desperately hoping that, somehow, I will find the answers to my questions in the letters she left for me.

Pulling back up into my mother's driveway after just leaving the night before felt like I was living here in her house again. It felt like I was returning home. After all, this was the house where it all began for me. This was the house where I first saw the image on the table that still sits in my mother's living room. The bedroom upstairs, my bedroom, was where the strange lady first held me against my will, and even forced me to see myself in the mirror on my dresser while I struggled to get free of her control over my body.

THE PULL

It's the bedroom where I saw, with my own eyes, the pages of my book turn all by themselves until they stopped on one particular page. It's the room that I awoke in after that strange man took me to that very unusual place the night when I was driving home from Birdie's prom. The things that were said to me while I was there that night, I can't even repeat now. Not until I can be sure I have them in a proper context in my own head. So I will have to push the events of that night far back in my mind while I'm trying to just get a handle on what it was my mother was trying to tell me in these letters. That night will have to just wait. Right now, I think it's best to take one thing at a time. And the first thing on the agenda was to read the letters!

You would think that memories, like the ones I have of this house, would cause me to never want to see this place again, yet this is where I feel I truly belong. If Rachael had experienced the things I have, she would be afraid to come anywhere near this house. She definitely wouldn't without performing one of her sacred ritual thingies first. But for me, all I can think of was getting to those letters that are concealed up in its attic.

After walking through the front doors, the bright light of day made everything inside appear a little different then what the low lights of the night before did. I can see now that the place could use some light cleaning. It would probably be a good idea to hire a maid to come in once a month to air out the place and to do some light dusting. If I did that, it would probably go a long way in helping to sway Birdie's decision about whether or not to move here. If I can show her that we can afford a maid to help with the cleaning, that should take care of her concerns about keeping the place clean. But that's something I can worry about at a later time. For now, getting into the attic was my only concern.

Although, the attic had a window at the far end, the light coming in only illuminated a few feet beyond the window. This small amount of light only helped to create an ominous atmosphere to the darkness that shadowed the rest of the attic. Light and shadow tend to play tricks on the human brain, and my nerves were already on a razor-sharp edge. So I hurried to get the lights on just in case it wasn't my imagination that was seeing someone standing in the darkness almost behind every rafter that was coming down from ceiling. Then I saw it, even more foreboding then the night before. The shoebox was still sitting where I left it almost as if it, too, was anxiously awaiting my return.

My mother had to have done a lot of planning, and she must have gone through a great deal of effort to make sure the circumstances were just right, so I would be the only one to find this box. Any number of things could have gone wrong that could have caused it to be someone else who could have discovered this shoebox sitting up here in the darkness for all these years. I'm assuming she must have placed these letters here years ago. How else can you explain that they're here now over a year after her death? Since no one knows the exact moment they will be leaving this life, she had to have thought this out well in advance. I think I'm beginning to understand now how much trouble she went through to ensure that I would be the one who would be the one to find them.

Almost for as long as I can remember, she warned us not to go up into the attic. She would use words like it's very dark and unsafe up there. She knew that these very words alone would pretty much guarantee that it would never be my sister to be the one to come up here. There was another thing she always did, now that I think about it, my mother made certain that when it came to my sister. I would always do the gentlemanly thing. I had to always make sure to hold the chair out for my sister to sit down at the dinner table. When we went out, I had to always help my sister with her coat, and when I was tall enough, I had to help my mother with her coat as well. Mom would say, "Raphael, these are the things a gentleman does for a young lady."

Now I get it. That's the real reason why she made me always sit in the back seat of the car whenever we went somewhere together. She was programming my mind to always look out for my sister. I think she suspected that this type of conditioning would predispose me to be the one to venture into this dark attic. It would be a natural instinctive reaction for me to want to protect my sister from any potential harm up here.

When I think about it now, there could have never been any doubt in her mind that I would be the one to come up into the attic and discover these letters. That's why she left them so conspicuously placed out in the open; she knew I would be the one to find them. I guess now I know why she left the house to both of us. She wanted to make sure the house would not be immediately sold upon her death, thus giving me enough time to discover her little secret she left for me up here.

Why though! Why did she go to such extreme measures just to be certain that I would be the one to discover these letters? Somehow, she must have known that one day I would be searching for answers. She must have felt that it was very important for me to know the information contained in these letters. What else can explain why she went to such trouble to see to it that it would be me up here and not my sister?

Since we never had another talk like the one we had that day, I'm guessing she must have concocted this complex scheme of hers as her back-up plan. She knew that one day she would no longer be here. She knew that the time for us to talk was running out, so she made certain that her death would be the reason for me to finally listen to what she had to say. I'm so sorry, Mom, it took me so long to get to this point.

I'm sorry that when you tried to talk to me, I didn't listen. If only it was possible now for you to believe me. It wasn't because I didn't want to hear what you had to say. It was because I couldn't listen to anything that seemed to me you were making more important than Dad. You and Rachael seem to have forgotten all about Dad so easily. But it wasn't that easy for me to forget him. I was hurt, I was angry, and I felt betrayed by you and Dad. Mostly angry at you because you didn't realized how much I missed him. Betrayed by Dad because he was gone, and he was never going to come back.

He left me all alone. I wasn't even a teenager, and he was already gone from my life. We never even got to do anything together. When Rache and I were little, you two would send us to spend the summer with Grandma Boot just so you could travel all around the world together. You promised that when Dad was promoted to the admiral's staff, which was the reason we moved to the Washington in the first place, you promised that we would finally be a family. You said Dad would come home from the Pentagon every night, and we would all be together and happy once and for all. But that wasn't the way it turned out, was it!

How could you expect me to want to continue to go to that church? Was I supposed to substitute religion for my father? Is that how you managed to forget him so easily? Was praying to the invisible God what made it possible for you to forget all about your husband and my father? I wanted my father back, and I didn't want to have anything to do with a church, a religion, or a God that would take him away from me.

Now you're gone too! And I never even told you the real reason why I walked away from religion that day. I think I even knew that I was also walking away from you that day! But I couldn't stop being angry at you for wanting me to forget about Dad. I'm sorry! I'm so sorry I didn't know how to tell you what I was feeling. I knew it wasn't your fault that Dad would never walk through the front door again, but I was only nine years old when Dad died, and he was the whole world to me, and I thought you wanted me to forget all about him! I know now that wasn't true.

You had to be strong for Rache and me. You had to keep us together. You had to make sure we made it to adulthood so we could take care of ourselves and each other. In my selfishness and anger, I didn't even notice what Rache saw so easily. You never remarried. You never dated another man. You never asked me to accept anyone else as my father. If only it wasn't already too late! If only you were still here, I could finally tell you the truth!

I could thank you for being the loving, caring, and understanding mother you were to me. And I could beg for your forgiveness! All these tears that I have held back and pushed deep down inside of me for all these years have finally found the reason to force their way to the surface. I can't hold them back anymore. Mom! I wish you were here! I wish you were still here with me now more than ever because I finally understand all that you did for me. But now it's too late!

CHAPTER 12

A Broken Promise

When I woke up, I was curled up on the plywood floor in my mother's attic. My clothes and face was covered with dirt. If I didn't know how I got this dirt on me, I would have thought I had been lying on the earth outside. Most of the day had already passed, and the sunlight coming through the window was now starting to fade. I must have been asleep for hours. I don't know what happened earlier. I know I didn't see it coming. Those emotions that poured out of me came as a complete surprise to me. I wasn't even aware that I was still harboring such intense feelings toward my parents. I knew these letters were supposed to help me understand the past, but I thought that it would be my family's history that would be elucidated, not my own life.

I feel silly now for crying like a little school girl while curled up in the corner of my mother's attic, thinking about the time when I was losing my religion and then falling asleep on the floor. I must have been really exhausted from not getting any sleep the night before. This was not the reaction I expected to get from the letters; especially since I haven't even read the first one yet.

It felt like something that had been kept bottled up, something I had blocked inside of me for a long time, was now opened. Whatever it was I experienced earlier, it seemed to have somehow freed me, or should I say released, something inside of me! I'm not sure what it was that I had just been freed from or what it was that had just been released, but I felt like a weight, weighing a ton, had just been lifted off my shoulders.

Thanks to this little episode of mine, I missed the meeting I was supposed to attend, and I have several calls from my foreman to return. That problem I can deal with tomorrow. If I was smart though, I would leave right now so I can make it home in time for dinner and have that talk with my son. But for the life of me, I can't seem to bring myself to do the smart thing. I have to know what all this mean. I can't leave out of this house without at least attempting to unravel this mystery my mother has asked me to solve.

I know that this will only make matters worse, but to call Birdie now would only mean that I would have to say things that I'm not ready to talk about with her yet. I can't bring her into this, not until I know exactly what this is. Not until I know what it is I'm dealing with. The only way I can find answers is to read. So, as instructed, I plan to follow my mother's instructions and read all the letters in the precise order of her arrangement. I will read my grandmother's letters first and then I will read my mother's.

I know that it is not humanly possible to read all these letters at one time, but I can at least start with the first of my grandmother's letters. But first, I'm going to have to get out of this attic and these clothes. Anyway, it's not enough light up here to read from, and there isn't a way to get comfortable unless I want to try to sit in one of those folding beach chairs. That's not going to happen!

The most logical place in this house to sit comfortably so I can read is the sofa in the living room. Then if the need should ever come over me again, I can use the sofa as a bed instead of the floor. There is no way I'm going to take one step into my mother's living room without cleaning myself up first. Once I'm down from this attic, I'll just use my bathroom to take care of that. Unlike my sister's bathroom in the guest quarters, my bathroom was designed to function to the needs of children. There is no fancy Jacuzzi tub in there. No marble tiles on the walls and floors. Just the regular four by four ceramic tiles on the walls of the tub surround and mosaic sheet tiles on the floor.

THE PULL

The color selection is also for that of a child. The field tiles in the tub surround is white but centered on each wall tiles are cut out in the shapes of diamonds so the four prime colors tiles can be inserted to form a green, a yellow, a blue, and a red diamond on all three walls. The green and yellow diamond-shape tiles were centered horizontally or east to west. The blue and red diamond-shaped tiles were centered vertically, or from north to south, making each wall have four different-colored diamond shapes that formed the outline of a larger diamond in their center. The two-by-two mosaic floor tile pattern was also white with the four prime colors randomly placed throughout. Everything in there seems much lower than I remember growing up, and the bathroom seems a lot smaller then I remember it being too!

I don't think that I will be able to find a change of clothes here; not any that can still fit me anyway. There should be an old loose-fitting sweat suit still folded up in the top draw of the dresser in my room. I left the top and pants here when I had to come over to take care of the place while my mother was in the hospital. It's funny how the mind works. Although, I know that my mother is no longer here to chastise me for going into her living room I can't help it; I have to make sure that I don't mess up her sanitized furniture. There has to still be some clean blankets and sheets in the hall pantry. I will use those to cover everything before I sit on her spotless sofa, and I'm going to make sure to throw a thick heavy blanket over the glass of that coffee table while I'm at it.

That reminds me, while I'm thinking about my mother's furniture, I need to call the movers so I can cancel the move that's scheduled for the end of the month. I'm sure the news that I've changed my mind about moving everything out of here will make Rachael very happy. I'm not so sure what that news will mean for Birdie and me though. But I think it best that these letters not leave this house. I can just keep coming here where I will have the privacy I will need without having to worry about being interrupted. That way, I will also be eliminating, as much as possible, the chance that someone else could accidentally discover the letters. Especially since that seems to have been a very important concern of my mother's.

The next thing I need to do is find a safe hiding place where I can keep the letters so I won't have to continue to go up into the attic to retrieve them. The only person I have to worry about accidentally discovering them is Rachael. No one else has any reason to be here, at least for the time being. I think the back of my mother's closet would be a good place to store them for a while. My sister isn't ready to deal with going through my mother's things yet, so this should give me a little time until I can find a more permanent hiding place.

Now that I have all the minor problems resolved, the big one—such as explaining to Birdie why I wasn't home in time for dinner—will just have to wait until I get home tonight.

CHAPTER 13

Letters to Her Daughter

Finally, I'm ready to take a look at the letters. I think the only way I will be able to resist the urge to go straight to my mother's letters is to leave them in the shoebox. I would really like to hear what she has to say about her and my father, but she must have had a reason for asking me to read my grandmother's information first. So the least I can do is to try to honor her last wishes, regardless to how difficult I may find this request to be. I wonder though, just how much do I really remember from the story my mother told me that day? How much do I really know about my mother and grandmother?

I know that my mother was born in North Carolina. Although she came from a very large family of five boys and six girls, she and her immediate brother were twins and they were the oldest. They were the children of her mother's first marriage, which was the polite way her mother and father's relationship, in the past, had always been described to me. My mother's name is Willamina and her brother's name is William. They came from a family of eleven children total, but as I stated, she and William were the children of her mother's first love. While telling me the true version of our family's history, my mother reminisced on how it was such fun having a brother with the same nickname.

With her being called "Willa" and her brother called "Will," when they got in trouble, which was apparently pretty often, for the pranks they played on their other siblings and friends, the cry was always, "It was the Wills that did it!" Also, with them looking nearly identical, they would sign in for one another when the other was tardy or absent from class. This was a private joke that only she and her brother shared, and this, she said, made them very close. Of course, after she reached a certain age, she informed me, their differences became too obvious for their pranks to continue. But during their early years, they were almost indistinguishable and inseparable.

For some reason, she didn't share the same closeness with her other half-siblings. She wasn't certain if this was the case because she and William had a different father, which made them look very different from the others, or if it was because of the stigma associated with her parents' relationship. My grandmother was a purebreed Cherokee Indian. What little I can remember from that day my mother had to say about my grandmother had more to do with her people then it did with my grandmother's actual history.

Her people, who were a part of the five civilized tribes, didn't make the move westward during the force migration as most of those from the Choctaw, Seminoles, Muscogee (Creek), Chickasaw, and the Cherokee Nations had done on the Trail of Tears starting in the early 1830s and ending in the year 1838, which was the year the federal government forced the last of the Cherokee Indians off their land so the land could become farmland for European settlers.

This was a difficult and treacherous forced march that covered nearly a thousand miles and covered the territory of Tennessee, Kentucky, Illinois, Missouri, and Oklahoma. Along the way, whooping cough, typhus, dysentery, cholera, and starvation were epidemics they would face, and it's estimated that more than six thousand Cherokee died making this march to what today is Oklahoma.

My mother said my grandmother's ancestors, however, were very proud people and they called themselves *Aniyunwiya*, which meant "principle people." Some of them didn't agree with the abandoning of their territory. They remained in Georgia and the Carolinas, the land of their forefathers. Fortunately for them, much of their territory was found in the Blue Ridge Mountains, which are a part of the larger Appalachian mountain range that extends from Georgia all the way into Pennsylvania. For many decades, they were driven away

THE PULL

from civilization—chased by federal troops for years until the pursuit was finally abandon from sheer exhaustion.

Forced to live a solitary existence among their own people high up in the mountains, where the earth and the clouds meet, they thrived living off what the land gave them. Over those decades, they had to endure much hardship and hatred, but they would eventually come to accept the offer of citizenship once the government determined this was a better approach then trying to chase them all over the mountain range. They could then be registered in order to be counted in the censors taken in the early 1920s. They would even come to accept the shameful title of "Assimilated Indians."

After a century of living high up on the mountain, the Thundercloud people, my mother's grandparent's name, moved down from the Blue Ridge Mountains and settled in Sumter County, South Carolina. I found it hard to believe that, at one time, there were people who actually sought out Indians for the purpose of making it rain. But as my mother continued her recapitulation of our family's history to me that morning, this was obviously the case. Long before, but especially during the decade of the nineteen thirties, which was the time America experienced the worst depression in its history, my great-grandparents (and their parents before them) would be repeatedly called upon to provide the service of rainmakers.

While the nation as a whole was experiencing the tragic result of the stock market crash of 1929, the cotton farmers of the South were being doubly afflicted because of the arrival of the boll weevil, which is a beetle that feeds on cotton, and it first appeared in the Carolinas as early as 1915. During the times of the Great Depression though, the boll weevil was ravishing the cotton crops of the South, and some even speculated that this was one of the contributing factors for the downturn in the nation's economy.

In any event, many of the cotton growers were losing their land and their homes. Those that didn't lose their homes became sharecroppers. This meant they would farm the land of the larger landowners for a nominal fee and in many cases, the land they were now farming for someone else used to belong to them. They were paid barely enough to keep their houses out of foreclosure while making the rich richer. This in turn caused a state of near panic for the other farmers in the South, for the corn, peanut, and soybean farmers especially. Rain became the most precious commodity, and they were willing to try anything to keep from losing their crops and land.

Some of these farmers, in their desperation, offered small portions of their hundreds of acres of land to certain Indians who were, reportedly, capable of making rain. Providing this service, and helping to work the land of their benefactor, while also supplying fresh meat and fish from their hunting, trapping, and fishing, these Indians were given back a small portion of the land that once belonged to their ancestors. This allowed these Cherokee Indians, of which my great-grandparents were among, to live on these privately owned farms without being harassed on their little piece of land secluded from everyone else. This harmonious coexistence between white farmers and Cherokee Indians would last for more than just a few decades.

Anyway, as I was told, this was how my great-grandparent's people first received the name Thunderclouds—for their alleged ability to make it rain. Although, my grandmother would say that it wasn't alleged. Her people actually did understand the science of rainmaking! Well, that's the history of my grandmother's people—at least as much of it as I can remember.

Now that I have the opportunity to read my grandmother's letters in her own words, I can finally fill in all the blanks and gaps in my memory from the day when my mother tried to tell me this story. It's already starting to get late, and I'm already in big trouble, so I might as well read the first letter since being a few more hours late won't make matters any worse than they already are. So, Grandma, what do you have to say that is so important that Mom wanted me to hear your story first? As much trouble as I'm in with Birdie, it had better be good!

An hour passed before I completed reading the first letter my grandmother wrote to my mother, and I immediately began reading the second letter she wrote to her. The second letter picked up right where the first letter left off. There was no indication of a break in the story. It just began in midsentence from the first letter. It was as

THE PULL

if once my grandmother started telling this story, she couldn't stop writing until it was finished. It took several letters before there was an actual break in her story. And I, strangely, found myself being compelled to continue reading her letters until she reached the end.

Wow! This really is a dozy of a story! In some ways, the information contained in her letters has helped with my understanding of my family's history, but in other ways, more profound ways, it has only served to make my story even stranger to tell. I don't even think it will be possible to tell my story now without first telling my grandmother's story. The best way, I feel, to do that is to simply tell the story as one letter. What took, for me, several letters to read, will be just one continuous story for you.

With the information she provided in her letters, I'm beginning to understand what it was my mother was trying to share with me that day of our conversation. But how can what I just read possibly be true? I've only read the first few letters, and it has changed everything I thought I knew. How could my family have played such a crucial role in shaping the history of this nation? Am I actually supposed to believe that these strangers, as my family seems to like to call them, have been involved with my family for such a very long time? Is this what the dreams are really all about? Is that why they have involved themselves in my life too? Am I really supposed to believe that they are showing me the role I will now have to play in shaping the future?

Since I'm now compelled to tell my grandmother's story, I feel the only way I can accomplish this is to try, whenever possible, to use her own words. I will try to write exactly what was said in the letters I just read. But some of the words and phrases my grandmother used just doesn't have any meaning today, and her writing in particular, although it is very beautiful, was also very difficult to understand. Her spelling was atrocious. This, I think, may have been due to the fact that she spoke broken English which combined her Cherokee language as well. Some words she used aren't fully Cherokee words nor are they really English either.

During her day, this may even have been an understood local vernacular, but trying to make sense of it today was just too taxing. Even the words I did recognized from growing up around my grandmother and mother would be too difficult for me to try to explain to someone who has never actually heard the words spoken in this unusual dialect. But I will try to explain some of those words with what I think were her intentions when they are pertinent to her story.

The words that I remember and can easily translate, I will also do so. Although I still could be wrong about some of her words. From the looks of her handwriting, I may have to rewrite whole sentences so the story she was trying to tell will flow smoother. If parts of her letters were clear and concise, just understand that I'm doing you a favor. Rather than have you spend several minutes trying to figure out what she meant, as I did, you will be able to read without frequently having to pause—hopefully!

I should give one more caution here before I let her words be read. These were letters between a mother and her daughter. They were letters one woman was writing to another woman, and some of the topics covered were of very personal aspects of womanhood. It's only because they engulfed events in such a powerful and meaningful way that I feel I have no right to change or try to alter the clarity and relevance they bring to the chronicle of the history of this nation. That's why I feel these words of my grandmother, although they may cover some painful moments of our past, should be allowed to speak for themselves, and it's my every intention to allow them to do just that. So it would behoove you to prepare yourself for some very shocking revelations.

They say the best way to understand another person's life is to walk a mile in their shoes. So I guess what my mother and grandmother were asking me, and now I'm asking you, when you read her letters is not to just walk a mile but to walk several hundred miles with her people. If you allow yourself to do that, you may feel, as I did, that you have a much deeper understanding of the plight of the American Indians than you had before. By the time you read her letter, it will still be my grandmother's story, but I would have changed many of the words, and perhaps been a little creative with the very vague and obscure fragments of the story she managed to put on paper. This way, I'm hoping, her letters will be more comprehensible.

THE PULL

Right now though it's almost time for the sun to come up. I think its best that I get home and face the music for my actions of the last day. Boy, is Birdie going to be upset. It's going to be a very long day! Will there be anything left of me when it's over?

THE FIRST RAY: EARTH—SURVIVAL OR FEAR!

CHAPTER 14

The Story of Wahketsi Begins

To Willa, my beautiful black pearl.

It's time for me to tell you the story of how your father and I first met. For a long time now, I have been wanting to tell you and William the truth about us. It ain't an easy thing to explain what we felt for one another, and how we met is almost as strange as why we met. But none of that is gonna make any sense until you first learn something about our family history. So before I can tell you that story, you must first know the whole story. So I'm gonna have to come back to the story of me and your father later.

Willa, since the time I was a little girl, I had already heard the story over a hundred times at least, about what happened to us when our people were forced off our land by the government troops. What you read in the history books today ain't the way the story was told to me when I was a girl living in our family circle (tribe) in the woods up on the mountains. My mother was the daughter of the chief, which means your grandmother was a princess; that also makes you to have royal blood in your veins. My father was the son of the *Ani-Kutani*. This means that your grandfather came from the wise priestly line of our people.

When my mother and father married, she had just lived fourteen years, and he was only seventeen and was already considered to be a brave (man) in our circle. They were to be the new leaders of our circle once it became time for the elders to travel on the sky journey (die). My mother's name was Moon Glow, and my father's was Morning Sun. When Moon Glow gave birth to twins, she was only nineteen years old, yet for my brother and me, we already had three older brothers and one oldest sister when we came into this world together.

It's not exactly true what the history books say about the Cherokee people. Not all our people changed to the white man's laws. Our circle never changed. We followed the way of the Sky Gods (traditional Cherokee beliefs). The *Nvda* (moon, I think), she taught us how to follow her circle (year or years) and her husband, the *Nvdo* (sun, must be), taught us how to grow food. Because the Moon shined her light (knowledge) on our people, the woman was in charge of all decisions that related to the circle. She chose her husband, and the husband became a part of her family or even her circle. The Moon taught her all the skills of womanhood. It was the woman with whom the Moon first shared the knowledge of her healing powers and medicinal herbs. The most powerful magic and healing first belonged to woman, only to later be shared with the medicine man. That way, the women would not be bothered while raising the children.

The light of the Sun taught our braves to provide food and protection for the circle, and they became wise in all the knowledge of nature and the earth. The Father Sun would impregnate the seed in the womb of Earth Mother, and she would give birth each year. My mother told me that's why our people are called the *Aniyunwiya* (the Principal People) because we formed our circle (village in this case) after the two great circles of the sky. The two great lights in the heavens: the Nvda (moon and sun)!

The Earth Mother lives in the center of the circle of the Sky Mother Nvda (Moon Goddess), and she measures the course of the Sky Mother. Earth Mother makes twelve counts the times she sees the Sky Mother's face (full moon). On the day of the year and on the night of the year, the Earth Mother divides the circle of sky mother in half. The Great Sky Father Nvdo (sun god) is in the center of the circle made by Earth Mother, and he makes seven counts the times he sees Earth Mother's face return (week). So as the space from Sky Father to Sky Mother is to the space from Sky Father to Earth

THE PULL

Mother, so is the space from Earth Mother to Sky Mother. We were not ignorant people. We received and accepted the knowledge the gods shared with our people with honor and reverence. These are the forgotten old ways that were taught to us when the gods visited us in the first time.

Willa, it was the women who passed down the history of the circle to their daughters, so as my mother did for me, and her mother did for her. I will do for you to the best of my recollection. When this story was first told to me, it was already almost a hundred years old, and I figure you can be sure some growth happened (embellishment) after all those years. But I don't think anything that weren't true had ever been added; only maybe, more details as whoever was telling the story saw fit. You ain't gonna read this story in the history books of white folks. They don't usually take too kindly to deserters that went against them when they be telling of their history.

I know this to be the truth on account that I wouldn't have been born if it weren't true, and if it weren't true. I would have never lived to see such a beautiful woman be my daughter. 'Cause it was your great ancestor, Wahketsi (Wah-Key-T-See), Nvda (daughter of twelve moons or daughter of mother of twelve moons).

Like I already said, I'm not sure why my grandmother spelled certain words the way she did. As far as I can tell, Wahketsi is not fully a Cherokee word, but my grandmother must have had a reason for choosing the words that she did. Maybe she used these words because she didn't want to say the real people names in her story—I don't know. All I know is that she kept associating this name with twelve moons. I don't know why, because nothing I remember about the Cherokee language supports that assertion. But I'm going to honor her by leaving her words the way she spelled them. When I can, I will try to give my interpretation of what I think she meant based solely on my grandmother's writings. The best interpretation I can give for this name is "daughter of twelve moons."

Wahketsi was your great, great-grandmother who lived to tell her story to our people. The story goes that way back in the first years of 1830s when the government troops started rounding up the Choctaws and claiming their land in what today is the land stretching from Florida all the way to Mississippi. The other Indian nations became divided. Most wanted to continue to trust in the treaties they had already agreed too with the states in which they resided.

Some wanted to trust the great white chief, Mr. President Andrew Jackson, on account that it was Indians that had helped him win many battles against the British and Spanish troops so he could claim the land Florida as his own (an American province). Indians would fight on both sides in those battles. The Cherokee, themselves, fought with the Army under Colonel Andrew Jackson in the Red Sticks War. It was Chief Major Ridge that led the Cherokee in battle. John Ross also helped in this war against the Creeks. But others remembered the wars General Andrew Jackson fought against the Seminoles Indians to force them off their lands, and they believed that it would only be some time before their land would be taken too.

Many powwows (meetings) would be held over the following years. At first the meetings were held in the capitol city for the Cherokee, New Echota (Georgia), but nothing ever got decided. When more and more white people were coming and taking over the Cherokee's land, the meetings had to be moved because then the Georgia state government started forbidden Indians from holding meetings anymore. That's when the meetings came to Red Clay (Tennessee). This place was chosen because it provided much shade, and the spring called Blue Hole was there, so there would be plenty of drinking water for the people, horses, and livestock. A council meeting house was built and other buildings for storage were built from the plentiful supply of trees the forest provided.

People from the Cherokee Nation came from many miles away to be at these meetings. Some came from as far as North Carolina. They came on horseback or in oxen-pulled carriages. Many from surrounding lands walked many miles just so they could hear what was going to happen to our people. Even the people of the mountain tribes came down to these meetings.

CHAPTER 15

Chief Iahoo Speaks at Red Clay

At the first meeting at Red Clay, John Ross, who was now the principle chief of the Cherokee people, spoke about the invasion of the white settlers into our lands. He wanted to continue to fight for our land using the white man's words in the courts. Most of the other chiefs agreed with him. A few secretly, including Chief Major Ridge, his son John Ridge, Elias Boundinot, and John Ross's brother, Andrew, along with a few other men, wanted to accept the white man's offer because they were promised that the Cherokee people would be given land in the new territory where they could be self-ruled. These men were a brotherhood and great friends of Andrew Jackson. But cowardliness, greed, wealth, or power are the real reasons why men betray their own people, and for those reasons, these men, whom some called traitors, would all eventually meet with a sudden and very violent death.

Only one chief, Iahoo, the chief of the mountain people who had come to the meetings with his wife, two daughters, and a small hunting party, stood up and spoke out against trusting in the white man's laws. Chief Iahoo was not dress like the other chiefs. His head was wrapped in the traditional bandana (turban) of the Cherokee chief, and it had one feather of the white owl stuck into the back. He wore the hunting shirt for the chief, which was made with an embroidering of many colorful beads of red, orange, yellow, green, blue, indigo, and purple. He had a beaded belt around his waist also embroidered with those colors and he wore deer skin leggings.

Now the mountain people spoke with the old tongue (language). Mostly the lowland people had been the ones to change to the white man ways and customs, and they dressed in the clothes of the white man. They could speak with the white man's tongue and some of them, John Ross included, could not speak the Cherokee language and had already forgotten the old words and the old ways. The lowland Cherokees had, for many moons, lived the ways of the white man. They made houses of wood and lived in towns also like the white man. They kept Negro slaves as also was the custom of the white man, and many of these Negroes would travel with the Cherokee on the force march to the new Indian Territory.

Chief Iahoo, with many of his words needing to be explained by his wife, Ahyoka, because she could speak a little of the white man's words, spoke out to remind everyone what happened to all the other Indian nations like the Creeks, the Choctaws, and others that trusted in the white man's laws. He reminded everyone how each one of those nations trusted and served with the great white chief in battle, yet they all still lost their land. Chief Iahoo still remembered the powerful words and could speak with the tongue of the gods. The gods are no longer happy with the Cherokee people, he announced, because we left them for the gods' of war.

"In the time, long before, all Indians were one people. We all came from one nation; we all spoke one language. Then the two great brothers became jealous of each other's kingdom, and they fought great wars that destroyed each other. Then the people started to move up from the land of the South, and we spread out all over the Northern lands. We forgot that we were once all brothers, and we fought each other and pushed away from each other. That's when we became different people speaking different languages and living different ways and customs.

"Now the time of darkness has come for our peoples because we are no longer worthy of the gods. As the ancestors spoke, the dark times would come, and the world would not see light again for many cycles of the moon to come. During the time of darkness, the way to truth would be lost, and only the way of ignorance would remain. The knowledge of the heavens would be forgotten, and Earth Mother

THE PULL

would weep and suffer. But the gods who visit us would also be fair; they will also visit the white man.

"The white man speaks with words like the little people (little spirits that trick people) and cannot be trusted. The ink on the white man's paper is written with words that are not straight but are always changing like the trail of a snake. Trying to trust the white man's words is like trying to hold a wet fish in your hand."

When Chief Iahoo was finished speaking that day, no one could say anything for several minutes because their hearts had been convicted by his words. Chief Iahoo was not a member of the council nor was he a leader for the Cherokee people. Many of the leaders and those members of the council didn't even know him. They had only heard of him by word of mouth. His words were not recorded that day, and they didn't make it into the history books, so they would soon be forgotten.

Then the time came for Chief Major Ridge and his group to speak at one of the meetings. Major Ridge's group were the ones who wanted to give up our land, and they had negotiated with the government without telling the other chiefs. He began by saying the Cherokee people should have accepted the money offered to us if we would have been willing to voluntarily leave our lands. He said this was a big mistake because in order to save the lives of the Cherokee people, he and the others in his group signed a treaty with the government. Then he read the words of General Winfield Scott. The general told the Cherokee people that he would be coming with a powerful Army to force them off their lands if they didn't leave on their own by two years' time.

Now John Ross and the other chiefs were very angry. He told Major Ridge that they had no right to speak for the whole Cherokee nation. Those who were there at this meeting swore that John Ross snatched the papers from Major Ridge hands and tore them up right in front of him. He said he would not allow this treaty to stand. All the other chiefs and those at the meeting were outraged by the news of this treaty. So that day, they all agreed that Chief John Ross had to continue to fight with the white man's words in the court of law even if he had to go all the way to Washington City again to do so.

They all agreed except Chief Iahoo, who, after this meeting, decided to stop coming down to powwows with the lowland peoples.

Also sitting in Chief Iahoo's party that day was his youngest daughter, Wahketsi. She was not yet sixteen years of age, but she already wore the eagle feather in her raven black hair. All the other braves her age wore the turkey feather in theirs. Wahketsi was very bright, and the understanding of the ways of war came natural for her. This is why she wore the eagle feather in her head because she could out do all the other braves in the war games, which consisted of shooting, throwing the knife, hand-to-hand fighting, fighting with the knife, and survival tactics like tracking, hunting, and fishing. But more than that, from a very early age, she understood the powers of nature and the ways of the witch.

She was born the daughter of great magic workers, her mother and father; both understood the power of the old words, so she was called "Twice the Powerful!" Some even say that in her later years, Wahketsi was the one who became the most powerful witch of all who was known to the Cherokee people as the "Raven Killer." When Wahketsi heard all the words Major Ridge, a man she had heard many great stories about growing up, and the other men had to say that day, she didn't show any anger like everyone else in the meeting. Instead, she remembered the names and the faces of every man that help to sign the Treaty of New Echota. While everyone else was outraged, that very day Wahketsi started planning her of revenge!

Now at the next meeting, everybody wanted to hear what Chief John Ross had to say when he came back from talking to the congress in Washington City. That day, John Ross looked like a man that no longer loved life. He looked like a man that could see his own grave, and when he spoke, his words were weak and soft. He didn't speak the words that helped the people to be confident in him. He did not speak with the fire of war in his words. His words were as soft as water running in a creek. His chest was not pushed out like a proud man returning from victory over his enemies. Instead, his posture was that of a broken man.

"I stand here today with a heavy heart and a troubled soul. As you all know, we went to Washington City with a signed petition of over fifteen thousand names to show the Senate that the majority of the Cherokee people did not agree to vacate their land as it is stated in the false treaty of Echota. We asked that the Senate overturn the law that made this treaty legal. Our request failed by one vote.

"Now we must decide whether to negotiate or to fight. We already hear of all the brutality that is being done to our people who refuse to give up their land to the government troops and the Georgia state militia men. To me, I now feel the time of war has passed for our people. It's now time to think about our survival as a people. If we continue to resist giving up our land, it will only hasten our destruction. The Cherokee people must survive!

"The Cherokee people must live on so those that have died protecting our land, and our ways won't ever be forgotten. There must always be Cherokee people who remember our history so we can tell our children, grandchildren, and great-grandchildren what happened on our lands. That's why I've decided to negotiate a peaceful removal for our people, so there will be no more bloodshed on our lands."

So in the end, John Ross agreed to honor the treaty the traitors signed. Some say that this decision saved our people from extinction. Others felt they would have rather died then to give up their land. This was the speech John Ross gave to the last of the so-called civilized tribes that Mr. Andrew Jackson (and now President Martin Van Buren) betrayed with help from those Cherokees that wanted money and power.

Even though the United States Supreme Court ruled that the signed treaty with the Cherokee people and the State of Georgia was legal, the treaty, which guaranteed that the Cherokee people would not be forced off their lands, was not honored. But the treaty that the conspirators, without Chief John Ross and the members of the council's knowledge, signed giving all the Cherokee land to the government would be honored. Although John Ross denounced this treaty the conspirators had signed with the government, congress used it to pressure the leaders of the Cherokee people to give up their land.

Willa, this is the way the story was told to me about all the events that led up to our people being forced off our land, and it had been passed down in our circle for generations. If it ain't the same way other people tell their story of these events, then I suppose they be telling it from their memory too. But anyway, that was the last time the Cherokee people met at Red Clay, and Wahketsi was there to hear the last words John Ross spoke at Red Clay. Here is how the story goes that explain why Wahketsi was at the last meeting at Red Clay, but her father Chief Iahoo wasn't.

CHAPTER 16

The Story of the Eagle and the Owl

When chief of the mountain people, Iahoo, wise owl, *doda Svnalei* (wise father of the morning or wise father owl of the morning), heard what was said at the meeting of the Treaty of Echota, he decided that he would lead his people high up and far into the woods of the mountains. Only his daughter, Wahketsi, doubted her father's decision to break off contact with the lowland tribes.

Now Wahketsi was headstrong and as brave as any man and would take offense if she was treated like a squaw (young lady). She used to like to hunt and fish with the other braves in the circle. Her hunting and tracking skills were better than any of the braves in their hunting party. Maybe if she would have been born in another time, in a time of peace for her people, she would have been different. But the times she was living in help to shape her attitude more than anything else.

She did not take to womanly things and had no interest in how she looked. She didn't care that she was very beautiful, and she didn't like to wear woman's clothes. Wahketsi wore men's leggings (type of pants) under her dress so she could hunt and fish with the other braves. When she painted on the war face, she dressed entirely in the clothes of the brave warrior. Wahketsi wanted to prove to her father that she was as good as a son 'cause the chief had no sons. His first wife, Wahetsi (*Wah-ee-t-see*) Nvda (mother of twelve moons), was Wahketsi's mother, and she died during childbirth.

His second wife, Ahyoka (she brought happiness), sister to his first wife, had not given him any children, but she was a mother already of a one-year-old daughter when they married. Her first husband, Ben Black Bear, was killed when the troops came with the settlers to protect those who were moving into the lowland people's territory, and he never got to see his daughter born. Although he was a son of the lowlands, Ben had married a daughter of the mountains, and he taught Ahyoka how to speak the words of the white man. It was also Ben Black Bear who taught the young braves how to shoot with the white man's riffle. When Wahketsi would become old enough to shoot, she learned to shoot a duck in midflight with just one shot from thirty feet away. She could also accomplish the same feat using a bow and arrow.

Ahyoka saw the little baby girl her sister Wahetsi left behind, and she took pity on her. She loved and care for Wahketsi just like she was her own daughter. She loved Wahketsi because she loved her sister very much. Without a mother to nurse her, Wahketsi would have died an infant, but since Ahyoka already had a baby girl and her milk was flowing, she shared her breasts with the baby girl of her sister. All the love she had for her sister she gave to Wahketsi. Ahyoka was the only mother Wahketsi ever knew, and Wahketsi loved her very much because she made her life very happy.

All the stories she remembered about how great and beautiful her older sister was, Ahyoka shared them with Wahketsi. She didn't want Wahketsi to ever forget her mother. Wahketsi's half-sister Woya (little dove) was a gentle soul, and although she was the oldest, she looked up to Wahketsi. Like all fathers, Iahoo loved his daughter very much, maybe too much. Because she was all he had left to remind him of his first wife, he would not force Wahketsi to do woman's learnin' but only hope that she would one day come to her right mind.

After a year of living up in the mountains without attending anymore of the powwows, Wahketsi spoke up to her father about his decision to flee into the mountains. "Is it cause of survival or is it cause of fear that you won't fight for our land?"

Chief Iahoo tried to talk some sense into Wahketsi's head. "Many of our people have already died that stood up to the government troops. Many chiefs have seen their sons and daughters ruthlessly murdered right in front of them. They have lost many braves in this war with the government, and they still lose their land in the end. I want to be the chief that try to protect his people and not see his children die."

Hoping that he could help Wahketsi understand why he made the decision he did, Chief Iahoo told his daughter the story of the eagle and the owl. This is the time when the two sky Gods wanted to create the two birds that would best represent their purpose and deliver their message to mankind.

"The Golden Eagle is a proud and mighty bird," he began, "with its seven foot wingspan. It flies so majestically high up in the sky that there is no challenge from any of the other birds as to who is the king of the daytime sky.

"The sun is its proud father, and he has blessed the eagle with the greatest eyesight of all. The eagle uses its great eyesight to hunt its prey. It can see a jack rabbit in an open field from over two miles away. Then it uses its tremendous speed to dive toward the earth, traveling at speeds over a hundred and fifty mile per hour swooping down and pouncing on its prey before it even knows what happened. So the eagle only hunts with the sun on its back, and this is how it has learned to feed itself. Its purpose is to deliver the message to mankind of the magnificence and power of the sun's energy. The last hunt of the day for the eagle is just before the sunsets. Once the sun has set, it returns to its nest.

"The Great Horned Owl is the silent and slow flying bird of the night and is the ruler of the night sky. The moon is its mother, and she has blessed the owl with special eyes that can magnify her light to help it see in the dark. She has also given the owl the sharpest hearing of all. The wise and cunning owl uses this excellent hearing to track down its prey in the dark. The owl perched on a tree branch seventy feet away can hear a mouse moving under a foot of snow. Then flying completely silent, it can find the mouse without ever even seeing it. Then it plunges its talons through the deep snow, striking the mouse before it even has a chance to react. Under the cover of night, with its silent wings and superb hearing, the owl hunts its prey. Its purpose is to demonstrate to mankind the wisdom and knowledge of the moon's energy. The last hunt of the night for the owl is early morning just before the moon sets and the sun rises. Once the moon has set, the owl returns to its perch."

"Wahketsi," the chief now calling his beloved daughter by her name to emphasize his point, "This is the balance of all life and all things. When there is balance, there is harmony and there is peace. Balance is truth! Where there is no balance, there is no truth. This is the forgotten code of the heavens, and it must be observed to preserve all life on earth. When the code is broken, the Sky Gods take peace away from mankind. Earth Mother becomes very angry with her children, and she sends plagues upon the people! Once things become unbalanced, there can be no peace."

The chief continues to explain the story of the eagle and the owl to Wahketsi with the hope that she will figure out the message it contains. "During the time when the eagle was still very young, it didn't understand its purpose. So one day, when the eagle was hunting, it saw the rabbit moving across a field. The eagle decided it would have the rabbit for dinner, but the rabbit saw the eagle's shadow growing bigger on the ground and knew that its life was in danger and fled away before the eagle could capture it. This made the eagle very angry with the sun. The eagle said to the sun, 'You made the shadow that warned the rabbit to flee, and now I must go without dinner today.' The eagle became so mad at his father the sun that it refused to hunt during the day.

"Now the eagle's eyes can't see that good in the dark, and it makes too much noise for the night time when it flies. So it could not surprise the rabbit in the night with its attack like the wise owl could, but because of the eagle, the owl could not find prey to hunt either. The eagle made so much noise that all the animals were afraid to come out of their hiding places during the night, and the owl could no longer rule over the night sky.

"All the rabbits became so happy that the eagle wasn't hunting them during the day. They stopped worrying and went out to eat and play. With their bellies full, they didn't even have to go out at night anymore. Fat rabbits with full bellies mean more baby rabbits. Each pair of rabbits became two pairs, then three pairs, then five pairs, then eight pairs, until there was thirteen pair of rabbits living in all the rabbit burrows throughout the land. There became so many rabbits living in the forest and roaming over the country side that soon there became a shortage of grasses and shrubs for them to eat.

"The squirrels hiding in the trees no longer fear leaving the trees to look for food on the ground during the day, so they also increased in numbers. The mice also no longer had to worry about leaving their holes in the ground during the day, so they began to rapidly multiply as well. The sparrows were no longer afraid to fly out into the open air during the day, and they multiplied as well.

"The sparrow said, 'Because the mouse eats seeds and small insects like we do, there will not be enough food for us to eat.' The mouse said, 'Because the squirrel eats nuts, seeds, vegetables, and fruits like we do, there will not be enough food for us to eat.' The squirrel said, 'Because the rabbit eats vegetables and fruits like we do, there will not be enough food for us to eat.' The rabbit said, 'The squirrel eats vegetables, the mouse eats the berries and fruits, the sparrow eats the ragweed and the grasses, that's why there is not enough food for us to eat: They are eating up all of the foods we like.'

So because of the fear that there wouldn't be enough food to go around, all the small creatures of the forest decided that they would have to go to war to determine who would survive. The sparrow said, 'We have the advantage of the air. We will strike the mouse from the sky.' The mouse said, 'We have sheer numbers. We will overwhelm the squirrels with our numbers by blanketing the earth.' The squirrel said, 'We can climb up into the trees. We will reign down our attack on the rabbit from the trees.' The rabbit said, 'We have speed. We will just outrun all the attacks and take the food we want in our wake.'

"For long periods of time, the mouse would rule over the forest. Other times, it would be the rabbit that reigned. Then the time would come for the sparrow to achieve superiority. Even the squirrel would rule over the forest for a while. The war between the small creatures of the forest raged on for many, many moons until one day, the sparrow sent out scouts to find a new place for food. The scouts flew very far but didn't find anything at first. The next time the sparrow sent his scouts even further away from the forest and told them not to come back until they find a new place for food.

"This time, when the scouts returned, one had blades of grass in its beak. Another had a live caterpillar between its beak, and the last one's beak was pinching a leaf that was so full of seeds they were pouring out the sides. The sparrows were so happy to see the food that they all started to sing and celebrate. When the squirrel heard all the noise the sparrows were making in the trees, he sent one of his spies to find out what they were celebrating. Now the spy for the squirrel while holding on very tightly underneath the branch where the scouts were making their report to the sparrow heard everything that was said.

"The scouts told of a land where there was plenty of food. This land was the land of man. On the land of man was a place where hay was kept and where seeds where being stored in open containers. The land had rows and rows of flowers growing on it where grasshoppers and caterpillars where there in abundance. The soil on the land was so soft that the worms didn't even have to bore deep into the earth to find their food. The land had trees planted on it with berries and fruit growing on them, and it had rows and rows of vegetables growing on another part of the land. It was the land of plenty this land of man!

"When the spy for the squirrel returned, he didn't want to discuss what he had learned while still in the trees for fear of the sparrows hearing, so the squirrels decided to talk on the ground. When the mouse saw the squirrels on the ground, he sent a spy to hear what they were talking about. Now the mouse had tunnels running in all direction just below the surface of the ground. So the spy for the mouse was able to hear everything the squirrels were talking about.

"When the spy for the mouse returned, he said, 'We should go underground so the squirrels won't know that we heard them.' Now the rabbit burrow was even deeper than the holes the mouse had made in the ground, so the rabbit heard everything the spy told the mouse. Because of this new discovery, all these creatures of the forest realized that a final great war was coming that would determine who would rule over the new land."

CHAPTER 17

Wahketsi Disobeys Her Father

So now Chief Iahoo, being finished telling his story, looked at his daughter and asked, "Do you understand the meaning of this story, Wahketsi?"

"No, Father! I do not understand the meaning of a story that sounds like it is a story for children. I'm no longer a child, Father, so don't talk to me like I am! I don't even understand why you would tell me a story like that while our people are being slaughtered and our land is being taken from us. Is this the story old men tell so they can justify their unwillingness to stand up to their enemies?"

"No, my daughter." Chief Iahoo was now showing his disappointment and bruised feelings on his face. "This story was told to me by your mother. She told me that on the day that I could tell her the meaning of this story, she would agree to marry me. I was only a few years older than you are right now when she made that promise to me, and although your mother was almost ten years older than me, she waited patiently for that day to come. She loved me very much, and I loved her very much. Your mother was very powerful in the understanding of the powerful words of magic, and she told me she would only marry a man that could understand the meaning of these words. By the time I was wise and mature enough to understand this story though, her health had already started to fail her.

"In spite of her failing health, she still wanted to give me a child. She said she didn't want to leave me here all alone without someone here that came from the love we had for each other. So we married, and from our love you came to be, and she ceased to be."

"I'm sorry, Father. I didn't mean to be disrespectful to you or to mother's memory. I don't want my actions to dishonor you, nor do I wish to bring shame to mother's name, but I can't think about the meaning of a story right now. I can only think about saving our people and protecting our lands."

"I know, my daughter. I know that right now all you can think about is the anger you feel. But anger is like burning kindle. It makes a lot of smoke until it burst into flames and consumes the wood. Daughter, don't let your anger consume you. Learn to control your anger and emotions. Don't let them control you! Channel them toward doing good instead."

"I will try, my father. I will try."

"Wahketsi, what's happening now to the Cherokee people, these things take time to understand. Wait for understanding. Be patient and the answers will eventually be made clear. Your mother waited for my understanding to come. Now I feel it's my time to wait for the love of our lives to come to understand the important lesson she needs to learn. Like your mother, I will wait for that day no matter how long it takes. You see, my daughter, you too are very powerful in the ways of magic. You will one day come to realize what your ancestors, and your mother, understood about the four creatures of the story.

"In the story, they represent the four elements—earth, water, wind, and fire. Your ancestors understood that these elements must remain balance. Our ancestors have been responsible for maintaining this balance since the time of the beginning, since the time of the "first time." You will know when you are ready to seek understanding. It will be revealed to you. You will be shown the meaning of the elements of the creatures in the story. The dream vision will be powerful, but don't be afraid when it comes to you. Wait—the stranger will come!"

Willa, the way the story goes, this is the answer Iahoo gave to Wahketsi. He was trying to teach her about the two paths of life because he knew that this was the only way she could come to understand her destiny. And he also wanted to protect her more than anything else. Wahketsi would not listen to her father's reasoning. Although she was still angry with him for not fighting for their land, she couldn't help but wonder about the meaning of the story of the eagle and the owl.

One thing she did understand about the story, or at least she thought she did, was that she knew because she wore the tail feather of the eagle on her head; the eagle in the story was her. She also felt that her father was the owl in the story because he wore the tail feather of the owl on his head. But that day, this was as far as she was willing to permit her mind to focus on solving the meaning of the story. Now that the story had been planted like a seed in her mind though; she would never forget it and would often return back to trying to solve its riddle.

For Wahketsi, it was the time of war, and for now she could only apply her attention to that subject. So later that day, she went to speak to the young braves that were in her hunting party. These were the young men that had done all the same training as Wahketsi, and they knew and respected her as a superior warrior. Even though they were all around the same age, Wahketsi spoke with words that they didn't fully understand. She always spoke as their leader, and they never questioned her leadership over them. She wore the eagle feather, so they all respected her for proving that she was a wise and brave warrior.

Wahketsi spoke of the duty and honor one should have to his people and to his nation. She spoke of the training they all had to endure in order to become the brave warriors they were. She said, "Our training and our lives mean nothing if we don't stand up and defend our land. This land is Cherokee. This land has always belonged to the Cherokee people, and it can only remain our land if we are willing to fight with our lives to defend it. We must be willing to die before we are willing to give up our land. Today, we are no longer hunters. Today we become warriors! A warrior puts his people and his nation first. A warrior is willing to die for his people. This is what I'm asking of you. Are you willing to die for our land?"

Wahketsi was still so very young, and she didn't seem to fully understand the forces that she so effortlessly controlled. Using only her words, she was able to bring the young braves into a frenzied state. They all became so excited that they all agreed they would follow her to their deaths. They created a circle with her in the middle, and they danced around her saying over and over, "You are the sun, where you shine your light we will follow. Wahketsi, she is the sun. Where she shines her light we will follow!" This was the first time that Wahketsi realized just how powerful her words were. As she stood in the center of the circle, she could actually feel the energy of each of the braves flowing through her. As this energy began to surge through her; she felt her own body begin to radiate with such power that she could not prevent from showing her exuberance on her face.

Later that night, Wahketsi and the young braves took their weapons and stole away back down the mountain so they could fight against the troops. Wahketsi was not yet seventeen years of age when she left the safety of the mountains, but by the time she attended the last meeting at Red Clay to hear John Ross speak at that final meeting, she already had much blood on her hands. She and her braves would already be responsible for many deaths of the government troops and the Georgia militia men. They were also responsible for giving many Cherokee back their freedom.

CHAPTER 18

The Gold Rush and the Cotton Gin

Willa, when the motivation is greed, the human brain can justify some of the most heinous acts of cruelty against humanity imaginable. When it was found out that gold was found on Cherokee land, and because the land that belonged to us covered millions of acres of land that could be used for farming, the government wanted to give this land to white settlers so it could be used to produce cash crops, with cotton being the chief of these crops because they now had a machine that could take the seeds right out of the cotton without making a fuss.

It's important, Willa, that you understand the real reason that your ancestors were forced off their land. Most of the stories about Indian uprisings and attacks on innocent people were shams so they could be used as justification to drive our people off our lands. Those attacks were usually retaliations for unprovoked attacks that had been done to Indians, their land, or their women. So let's get that part of the story straight first. Whenever Indians would fight back to protect themselves, government troops would be sent in to stop the attacks. This back and forth went on for a long time, until it was decided that the Cherokee must be removed from their land.

So with the promise of receiving millions of acres of farmland and the chance to strike it rich by mining the gold on our land, the government and the settlers coveted the land that had been promised to remain the Cherokees. It is believed by almost every Cherokee that not only were the troops promised rewards for every Indian scalp they captured but also that they were promised acres of Indian land for helping to drive us from our homeland. So some of the very men that would be the tormentors of our people were also going to be the ones who would inherit our lands.

There was one officer of the US Army that didn't want our land. He had no stake in removing us from our homeland. So his eyes were not cloud, and his heart had not been snake bit (filled with poison or greed) but was pure. And it turned out, he was also a very good man. He said he only came to our land on account of him following orders. He was from up North, and his family was from the Boston Territory.

He said he was one of the first to have been especially trained in Indian warfare tactics, and this is what brought him to our lands. His name was First Sgt. Luke Pagent, and he had never seen a real Indian until he arrived in our land. Everything he had learned about us came from studying the reports that came to him, and he said that the next step in his training was to get field experience. That's why he was sent to our land.

He himself didn't look like the other government troops. His hair was blond and his eyes were blue as the sky in go (spring). He had no hair on his face. His skin was clear and smooth, and he talked with the most perfect words (accent) of the white man. His head reached over his horse's shoulders (at least six feet). He stood tall over most of the other troops. Since he was trained to fight Indians, his first order was to kill those Indians that were called the Death Raiders who were attacking the camps at night and killing troops on the roads that were bringing the Cherokee to the camps. Then he was to help lead over a thousand Cherokees to the new Indian Territory.

This part of the story goes that it was Wahketsi and the braves that came with her from the mountain that became known as the Death Raiders. Wahketsi figured out that the government strategy was to win every conflict with sheer numbers. Most times the troops outnumbered the Indians, so they could take more casualties and still win. She also saw the mistake of her people's strategy. Since the Indians were fighting to protect their land, that made them a stationary target. Even when they did win a battle, they would have suffered

THE PULL

many deaths. The government would just send more troops to pick up where the other troops failed because the Indians would still be living on their land. They would be sitting targets that had already lost many braves in the battle before.

Wahketsi saw that the troops had to divide up into groups so they could take the Cherokee to the new Indian Territory. She saw that the camps could be attacked at night because only a few guards watched out while the other soldiers slept. She never attacked the same camp but would change to a different camp each attack. This made it very difficult for the troops to know which camp would be next. The Cherokee people would be rounded up and taken to Fort Wool in New Echota (Georgia). From there, they would be taken mostly by road to Rattlesnake Springs (Tennessee), which was about four miles south of Charleston City.

The camps are where they would bring the Indians after they forced them out of their homes. The Cherokee were not allowed to take any of their possessions from their homes because the troops feared that they could turn anything into a weapon. They would make the Cherokee watch as their belongings were first looted by the militia men, and then the rest thrown outside so it could be burned right in front of them. Then they had to witness their homes being moved into by white settlers before they were led away to the camps.

First Sergeant Luke Pagent would later tell our people that all that was done so it could have a psychological effect on the Cherokee people. After witnessing all their possessions being destroyed and their homes being occupied, the Cherokee would only feel hopelessness and despair about ever returning back to their land. Still, since the soldiers feared keeping too many Indians close together, the camps where spread out miles apart. Some of the Cherokee were taken to Army forts and some were taken to be kept in Army outpost, but most had to be kept in makeshift camps that provided little to no shelter from the sun, rain, or the cold. These camps were spread out just over the Georgia and Tennessee border.

CHAPTER 19

The Warrior and the Ghost Spirit

One kills to defend her homeland. The other kills because he is following orders. Two warriors that, as fate would have it, were being drawn toward each other in battle. Willa, who really knows the circumstances or the reasons why love strikes when it does? Or the real role destiny plays in the lives of great people? How much of what happens to people is their own doing, and how much of it is the purpose of the gods? Only the gods could have shaped all the events that would have been necessary for these two very different people, who were born from different worlds and came from different parts of the country, to meet. How else can you explain why two enemies, whose mission it was to kill each other; would fall in love instead? They might as well have come from different planets because they had so little in common. But first, they would have to survive their first meeting.

Willa, here is where it becomes important for you to pay close attention. This is the part of the story that is the whole reason why I'm even bothering to tell you the history of our people in the first place. This is where the stranger appears to one of our ancestors for the first time. I've been told this story so many times; I know each word by heart. I should—I have always been told ever since I was a little girl that I look exactly like Wahketsi. They say that I'm her image reincarnated, so when we were little children, we used to act this story out when we played, and I would always play the part of

Wahketsi. So you're just gonna have to forgive me if I sound like I'm speaking for her.

It was still early evening, and it was just before Wahketsi announced the new plan she made for the attack on the camp that night. The light of the sun was almost gone from the sky. The way the last of the sun's rays reflected off the clouds made them look like blood-red puffs of cotton. Wahketsi looked up at the sky and said, "The sky gods want the blood of our enemies to be sacrificed tonight. They are no longer satisfied with just the blood of the troops alone. They want the blood of the little chiefs (officers) tonight."

In the past, the Death Raiders would quietly kill the guards on duty during the night so no one would know until morning that they had been there, or they would set an ambush for the troops on the roads that were bringing the Indians to the camps. Once these Cherokees where freed, Wahketsi would tell them in her language to flee into the mountains. Some would understand, but most did not, and they would all eventually be recaptured.

"No matter how many guards we kill," she continued, "new ones are standing on post the next night. We are going to stop killing the troops only and start killing the little chiefs (officers) too. They have many troops, but not many little chiefs. The gods want the blood of the chiefs who have brought this plague on our land. Tonight," she told her braves, "the Sky Mother (Moon Goddess) will use powerful magic to make it possible for us to enter into the camp without being seen."

"It will be their blood that will be sacrificed to the earth mother tonight. We will no longer only attack from outside the camp, but we will sneak into the camp, and we will sneak into the tents where the little chiefs are sleeping and kill them in their sleep." When Wahketsi spoke, she spoke with powerful words, and all the braves were so moved by her words that they started shouting and doing the war dance.

Before they would attack a camp, they would watch all the movement of the camp the week before. They would watch from the trees, from the bushes, or even sometimes from being buried under grass and brush just outside the camp itself. This required great skill and tremendous patience. The first night you would come with stalks of tall grass tied to your back so you could lie down in the tall grass. You could only get this close to the camps at night, so once you were concealed, you had to remain on the ground until the next night. All this had to be done without getting noticed by the guards on duty.

Wahketsi wanted to make sure she knew everything there was to know about the camps before she attacked. So she would often be the one to attempt this very dangerous mission. It was so dangerous because she couldn't take any weapons other than her knife with her. She couldn't take any food for fear of a dog or animal smelling it and digging up her hiding place. She could only take drinking water, and she had to rub herself down with mud and roots so she would smell like the earth and the grasses covering her.

As it was before, Wahketsi would stake out this camp the week before the attack. The camp was in a clearing that had trees surrounding it on three sides. The trees acted like a natural fence around the camp. Just behind the trees in the back, and on both sides of the camp where the Indians were being kept, was a cliff that dropped several hundred feet to the sharp rocks below. So any attempts to escape the camp would usually end in death on the rocks.

The road that leads into the camp was also the only road that leads out of the camp. On both sides of this road was the tall grass that provided the cover she needed. From her well concealed vantage point, Wahketsi could see right into the camp, and she learned many things about where everything was in the camp. She saw that the officer's tents were located in a straight row on the left side of the road into the camp, and the troop's tents where on the opposite side of this road. The rear of the camp is where the Cherokee people were being kept; meaning their only route of escape was to run toward the cliffs.

Some of the men who had tried to escape beforehand were tied, but the women and children were not being restrained. Families were huddled together in small groups, and other families from the same town huddled together with them, making larger groups of people who knew each other. Even though they were all Cherokee, they didn't all come from the same place. They didn't all know each other, and they all weren't friends. Some spoke with the old tongue, and some spoke with the white man tongue. At night, there were only two guards watching over the Indian stockade and two watching the entrance into the camp. Wahketsi was in this hiding place the day the new little chief (First Sgt. Luke Pagent) rode into camp for the first time with three other soldiers.

Willa, of all the thirteen or more campsites he could have been assigned to, was it just coincidence or was it fate at work that would time his arrival to this particular camp, at this particular time when Wahketsi had already chosen this camp to be the one she would attack? For Wahketsi, seeing First Sgt. Luke Pagent for the first time, as she peaked from under the grass that covered her, brought strange sensations to her body. What had lain sleeping inside her for all her nineteen years of life was suddenly being awakened. She had never felt any urges of womanhood before, and she couldn't understand what it was she was feeling. She had spent all her life around men. Every brave with her, she had known since they were children, and she had never felt anything like what she was feeling now for any of them. She and the braves with her were all from the same circle, and in her mind, they were all her brothers.

First, she thought this new little chief must be a spirit because when she saw him, her heart began to pound in her chest. Hiding under all that covering made her heartbeat sound so loud to her, she was worried that the sound would give away her hiding place. She had to calm herself and bring these newfound feelings under control. Later that week, she thought, maybe he is a powerful medicine man who can cast magic spells because she could not stop thinking about him.

He was on her mind the whole week leading up to the attack on the camp. She felt she still wanted to kill this man, but first, and for reasons she couldn't understand, she had to see him up close. She still felt anger and hatred toward the white man for killing her people and taking their land from them, but she didn't feel the same anger or the same hatred for this man, and she had to know why he made her feel so strangely. This more than any other reason was why she changed from the very safe strategy of killing only the guards on duty to the very dangerous strategy of going into the camp.

Willa, years later when she told this part of the story, Wahketsi swore she felt this new little chief had tied an invisible rope to her heart and was pulling on the rope to bring her into the camp. She had always been a very wise and brave warrior, and she had never made a mistake in battle. Until that night, neither she nor any of her braves had ever been injured, captured, or killed. But this night, all that was going to change. All because she had to see this man up close before she killed him. Or so she told herself.

It was now starting to get late into the evening, and the moon would not shine during the time she planned her attack on the camp. Wahketsi knew this was the night the Sky Mother, Earth Mother, and the Sky Father would become one. So as they were about to leave their camp, she shouted out, "This is the night the moon turns to blood. Tonight, the moon will disappear from the heavens, and it will not return full for over two hours. This will be the time we will strike. It will be the time for us to take our vengeance. It will be the killing time. It will be the time of the blood sacrifice!"

It was an early mid-October night, and the air hadn't yet changed from the cool nights of autumn to the much colder nights of winter. Their breath did not make the smoke come from their mouth yet. The first snow hadn't fallen yet either, which would have made entering the camp much easier. The autumn leaves had just begun to fall to the ground. They were not yet so dry that they made much noise when you walked. Still, the little sound they did make made what Wahketsi was attempting to do that much more difficult. If they weren't careful, their footsteps would be heard long before they were even close enough to the camp to complete their very dangerous assassination attempts.

But Wahketsi knew that it would only be a few more weeks before the force march of her people would begin again. She knew that once the troops started to march her people away, it would be too dangerous to attack the troops from fear of her own people being killed. If she was going to prevent anything from happening, it was going to have to be tonight, and she would have to kill the little chiefs in order to change their plans. She thought to herself, *Even if it means*

THE PULL

I have to also kill the one that makes me feel so strange, I'm willing to risk everything if it means stopping my people from being forced off our land.

She had already assigned each of her braves a tent where she knew, from her observation, an officer would be sleeping. She made certain that the tent she assigned to herself was the one where the ghost spirit slept. She called him this name because of his blond hair and because she didn't think a human man could cast such a powerful spell over her heart.

What Wahketsi didn't know, in fact she had never even considered it, was that the braves that followed her did so because they were all in love with her. Each one would have willingly died to protect her from harm, but none loved her more than her best friend Galiqugisun (seventh sun or maybe she meant son). It was Galiqugisun who was assigned the tent where the captain slept because the captain was a very big man, and Galiqugisun was a powerful young warrior. He was alpha! And yet, even though he feared for Wahketsi's safety because he secretly thought this mission to be too dangerous, he was too afraid to say anything to her.

That night, all the tents were dark, which meant that all the officers were asleep, but there was one tent where the lantern was still burning. It was the tent of the ghost spirit. As it had been the case in the past, each brave was to kill the person they were assigned, and then take his weapon and ammunition. This is how the Death Raiders got their name because they would only take from the person they killed. When Galiqugisun saw that the lantern was still on in the tent where Wahketsi was to go, he did not go to the tent he was supposed to but instead followed Wahketsi.

When Wahketsi stalked down her pray, it would have been easier to hear a mosquito in flight ten feet away, then it would have been to hear her coming toward you. She moved with such stealth, she was nearly invisible. Her ability to move in the shadows while completely silent made her a lethal assassin. The tent where the ghost spirit slept was much bigger than those the troops used. He was given the tent that was used for meetings since he was only going to be in camp for a short time. Wahketsi was inside the tent without making a sound or casting a shadow from the lantern. She slipped under the skirt of the tent crawling on her belly with her knife clutched between her teeth.

Once inside the tent, she saw that the ghost spirit had fallen asleep while reading at his table. She crawled under the table so that when she rose up, her shadow would be covered by the shadow the ghost spirit was already casting on the wall of the tent. She only needed to get her knife to his throat, but he had made this a little harder for her to do by resting his head on the table top. She would not have to stand fully erect to accomplish her mission, but she would have to be face to face with him in order to deliver the death stroke.

Once she managed to make sure the two shadows blended together as one, she removed her knife from her lips and stared straight into the face of her target. She knew she only had a few seconds to remain in this awkward crouched over position before her body would make an involuntary twitch. A few seconds was all she needed, but several seconds had already past and her knife was still motionless. She had yet to do what she came to do. She was just staring into his face and trying to make sense of the feelings that where now controlling her actions. And then it happened! She either breathed too hard against his skin or a sudden movement of her body disturbed his sleep—he opened his eyes!

The shock of seeing a red-painted face staring at him only a few inches from his own caused the first sergeant to push away from the table. When he pushed away from the table with such force, it caused the folding chair he was sitting in to collapse and tumble over backward creating a loud noise for that time of night. Instead of fearing for her life and fleeing from the tent, Wahketsi laughed. While First Sgt. Luke Pagent was crawling around on his hands and knees trying desperately to get to his holstered gun hanging from the post by his sleeping cot, he heard Wahketsi laughing at him.

The sound of her laughter, the sound of her very voice itself, caused such a feeling of calm and peace to come over him that he no longer feared for his life. Just as he reached his gun, he no longer had any desire to use it, but he only wanted to turn around and see the figure that he was now sure would be that of a woman.

THE PULL

Galiqugisun, hearing all the noise coming from the tent, and fearing the worse for Wahketsi, rushed into the tent in a blind rage with his knife drawn in hand. First Sgt. Luke Pagent, now completely befuddled, felt an unexplainable surge of male gallantry to protect Wahketsi from the savage that had just burst into the tent. He fired his side arm, hitting Galiqugisun just above his heart, sending him reeling backward through the flaps of the front of the tent.

In that instant, reality came crashing down on both of them. Wahketsi suddenly realized that her best friend had just been shot because she didn't do what she was supposed to have done. She ran from the tent and helped Galiqugisun to his feet. They then hurried back into the woods and disappeared from which they came. For First Sgt. Luke Pagent, realization came in the form of him realizing that he should have reloaded his gun and chased after Wahketsi, but he couldn't bring himself to do that. For the moment all he could think about was the sound of the voice of the woman that made the laughter he had just heard, and he was enchanted by it.

CHAPTER 20

Captain Buford "Bumpy" Hastings

It was the captain who was the first to reach the first sergeant's tent.

"What the hell just happened? What are you shooting at this time of night?" Now Captain Buford "Bumpy" Hastings's words took longer to say than most folks (he probably spoke with a Southern drawl), and he was round in the middle from all the good Southern cooking his mammy (Negro slave) fed him.

He would often joke about how good nigga cooking tasted and would brag about how Beulah Mae, his mammy, made some of the best dinners in the South with her famous fried chicken seasoned with so many herbs and spices that each bite was an explosion of flavor in your mouth. Her mashed potatoes were so creamy, it was like eating sweat butter, and the aroma from her savory gravy was so good, you could taste it in your mouth. And how she simmered her collard greens with succulent pieces of pork fat, so tender and juicy, that each spoonful passed through your mouth without even needing to be chewed. Her lace cornbread was so good, it tasted like cake.

His two favorite things that he bragged about the most, though, were her iced tea and her dessert. When Beulah Mae made iced tea, she sweetens it with honey not sugar. This meant that the honey had to be added to the tea while it was still hot. The honey would completely dissolve in the tea so that when it cooled, every sip would be just as sweat as the last. Unlike adding sugar to tea that is already cold, the sugar just sits on the bottom of the glass and has to be repeatedly stirred up. With a glass of Beulah Mae's homemade iced cold lemon sweet tea, you never had that problem.

Oh, how much he loved to brag on her chess pie she made for desert. He would say that her chess pie was nothing but mostly sugar, eggs, and butter, but you ain't never tasted them together like they tasted in Beulah Mae's pie. He would say that her chess pie was so deliciously sinful, even Jesus couldn't resist having seconds. He would go on and on about how all her pies were so perfect when they came out of the oven that, had she been a white woman, she would have won a blue ribbon at the county fair. He would say that's why his uniform fitted him so tightly because he was born too privilege and had grown accustomed to eating good cooking.

And that's why people called him Bumpy; he looked like a pine cone with a head, two arms, and two legs sticking out. He wasn't a bad looking man in the face though. His face might have been considered handsome if he wasn't so fat. He would often wear bifocal glasses so it would make him look distinguished and intelligent, but looks can be deceiving. He wouldn't allow his men to call him Bumpy.

Only the people from Macon, Georgia, where his family already owned one of the largest plantations in the state, were allowed to call him that. It was because of his family's wealth and influence that he became a captain in the Army. They believed should he ever decide to have a political career, a military record would serve him well. Since his position of captain was only for show, he had never actually served in any battles.

When everyone else finally reached the tent of the first sergeant, that's when it was first noticed that none of the other officers were there, and also, that none of the men who were on guard duty had showed up either. Captain Buford had heard all the stories of the Death Raiders, and how no one who has ever seen one of them has ever lived to talk about it. Because his camp hadn't been attacked yet, he feared the Dearth Raiders more than any of the other conductors assigned to the camps. When his men came back and told him that all the officers had their throats cut in their sleep and that all the guards on duty were dead from being shot in the heart with arrows, he looked at the first sergeant and said, "You had better start talking and you better be quick about it."

Fighting desperately to bring his emotions under control, the first sergeant decided, he being a much younger man than the captain, it would be best to formally address the captain about this matter since he had only been in the camp for a week, and he had not had any time to establish a relationship with the captain and the other officers. So he didn't want his remarks to carry any emotions one way or the other.

"Sir, I fell asleep at the table reading over the map you gave me of all the camps and all the roadside attacks that had been done by these Indians. I woke up when I heard a noise. I looked up and there was one of them coming in my tent with his knife already drawn. I reached my pistol before he got to me, and I fired one shot. I hit him high in the chest. He fell backward out the tent. By the time I reloaded my pistol and went to check, he was gone. All that was left of him is the blood on the ground that you see, Captain, sir."

"Yeah, you asked me to draw you that map 'cause you said it was going to help you figure out where the next attack was gonna happen. Well, I guess we don't have to worry much 'bout trying to figure that out anymore now, do we! Boy, you either the luckiest dang fool to ever be born, or they do some mighty fine training up there in the North." The captain had no idea just how lucky he himself had also been that night.

"I got almost a thousand of them Ingins kept up in this camp, and more is supposed to be coming in a few weeks' time. It's all me and my men can do just to keep them fed with a turnip and a biscuit or when the cooks are fortunate enough to get some cornmeal, they get a piece of cornbread, and they get two cups of water a day to drink, one in the morning and one in the evening. Then we got to make sure they each got a blanket to keep warm at night. If that ain't already enough, we have to worry about them fighting amongst themselves, and we have to try to keep as many as possible from run'n off every chance they get and fall'n to their deaths off the cliff behind the woods.

"That's why I used my family's influence to request for someone like you to be sent out here to fight those wild savage beasts that have been attacking the camps. I knew they would be coming for this camp sooner or later. No one has ever even seen one of them Death Raiders, and now you gone and put a slug in one of them. All these men who died here tonight were my friends, and they were fine Southern gentlemen. They believed, like I do, that we are fighting to preserve the Southern man's way of life. When I say Southern man, I mean white man not the niggas or the Ingins have any claim to the South. This land was given to us by God, and by golly, we aim to keep every hard fought inch of it.

"We down here know all about how some of y'all uppity Northerners talk 'bout how we ignorant Southern folk treat niggas and Ingins. We know all about how some of those folks in congress, like that David Crockett fella, fought so hard to keep us from taking this land from the Ingins. But somebody up there was looking out for us simple ignorant white folks, and we both know who that is. He is a true brother of the order and a great friend of the South. They made sure David Crockett got his though, didn't they? He even got it by the hands of the people he fought so hard to help. That's what y'all might call poetic justice, but we down here call it Southern justice. It really is kinda poetic though when ya think about it. Aint it!

"Even the Supreme Court try to say that this land belong to them Ingins because they were here first, but them savages don't even know the value of the land they fighting so hard to keep. They walk around with gold tangling from their clothes while their children use gold to play with. They talk about nature and the earth like it's a living thing that must be respected. Folks with beliefs like those will never be able to prevent their land from being taken from them by industrious-minded people. People who have a divine purpose. People of vision who see what must be done in order to build a strong and powerful nation!

"That's the way of the world, son. The strong will always conquer the weak. And let me tell you something, boy. Aint nothing stronger than the determination we southerners have to provide a comfortable lifestyle for our families, and that's something all y'all up North need to get into y'all head. So I hope you ain't one of them Northerners, and if you do got any of those uppity ways in ya, then you better keep your mouth shut and learn to hurry up and follow my orders!"

In recounting the events of the night, the first sergeant had conveniently omitted the part about him waking up to find a knife at his own throat, and the part about it being a woman who was the one holding that knife. He was only too happy that the captain was on a rant about the virtues of the Southern man, and he chose not to mention that David Crocket died at the Battle of the Alamo fighting against the Mexican Army and that, although, they may look similar, the Mexicans and Cherokee where not the same people. They didn't even speak the same language. Apparently, though, to the Captain, one Ingin was no different than any other Ingin. All Ingins looked alike!

The first sergeant thought, since the captain had already addressed himself as being ignorant, he didn't think it would have been a good idea to confirm that for him. He also chose not to take offense to the tone and the clear threat in the captain's words. He was just relieved that the captain's fear; which was what was really causing this swell of emotional pride, had caused him to neglect to check his firearm to see if it had been reloaded as he had said.

"First Sergeant, I want you to get your men and go hunt them animals down and kill each and every one of them. If one of them is hit, then he is leaving a blood trail to follow. We may never get another chance like this again."

"Begging the captain's pardon, sir! But the first sergeant feels it would be suicide to hunt them at night. Sir, since they are the experts of the night, the sergeant asks permission to take up the hunt at first light? The trail will still be fresh.

"Once we get them on the run, they will be tired from being up all night. Sir, my guess is now that one of them is injured and maybe even dying, he will slow them down. So they will try to keep on the move all night so they can get as far away as possible from this camp before daybreak. That means they won't be able to rest until daylight. Then the daylight will become our advantage, and as long as we stay hot on their trail, more and more they will lose the advantage of the night, Captain, sir!"

"Well, if that's what all your fancy training tells you to do, then do it. Just remember one thing—a week from now, another group of those Ingins will be moving out. Then a few weeks or so after that, it will be our turn to move our Ingins to their new homeland. There have already been too many delays. There was an attempt tried to move some of them Ingins in August, but the drought had dried up all the streams for miles, so the attempts to take the water routes had to be abandoned. Then there was all that negotiation that went on with that John Ross fella and the general. Now General Scott tells us we got to let them pick some leaders from their groups so they can help lead their people so they can be the conductors. All we supposed to do is be overseers of this human train now.

"We don't have an option. We have to leave when our turn comes up, or it will mess everything up for everybody else to move their Ingins. I'm now short on officers, and it's gonna take awhile for me to get some more men in here, so I want you back before three weeks' time. But when I see your face again, if I see your face again, I want every one of those Death Raiders to be either dead or captured. When I leave this godforsaken place, I want to know that the death of my friends have been avenged or that you died trying to avenge them. Do I make myself clear?"

"Yes, sir! Very clear, sir!"

Now that was the story First Sgt. Luke Pagent told our people of how the night went after he saw Wahketsi for the first time. He wasn't sure if what he said to the captain about going into the woods at night was because he feared chasing after her in the dark or if it was because he was more afraid that she might have gotten captured or killed. The one thing he felt he was certain of, though, was that the captain fully believed he was sending him on a suicide mission, and that the captain never expected to see him again.

The captain didn't want his men to see just how afraid he was about what happened. He didn't know why the Death Raiders missed his tent, but he was really afraid they would come back for him. This is why he wanted to hurry up and send the first sergeant on this mission. He felt that as long as the first sergeant was chasing the Death Raiders, they couldn't come back and finish what they started, and he could sleep without worrying about waking up with his throat cut. For the rest of that night though, Bumpy didn't fall asleep but sat up all night on his cot in his pajamas wearing his bifocals and his pistol ready by his side.

CHAPTER 21

Daughter of Twelve Moons and First Sun of Cherokee

Death Raiders was not the name Wahketsi gave to the braves of her war party. That name was given to them by the white man. This was the thought that was on her mind as she moved through the darkness of the forest. She thought, *By now the others should already be back at their hidden mountain camp.* They never left the scene of an attack together but would all go separate ways. This would confuse anyone who was trying to follow them, and it made it easier for each of them to make sure they wouldn't lead anyone to their camp. So she knew that not only did she have to get Galiqugisun back to the camp by herself, but she had to also make sure they weren't being followed.

While she was struggling to support the weight of Galiqugisun on her shoulder and trying to hold her hand over his wound to stop the bleeding, she thought about if he were to die, what it would mean to their group. It was Wahketsi who came up with the name for their war party. She thought, since it was seven of them, she would use the Cherokee numbers, and each of them should be called by one of these numbers.

Since they were fighting for the survival of the Cherokee people, and she was determined to never allow the sun to set on the culture and history of the Cherokee people; they should also be called the suns of the Cherokee. So she gave herself the war name *Sowosun* for "the first sun" because she was the leader. Then there was Talisun for the second sun, Tsoisun for the third sun, Nvgisun for the fourth, Hisgisun for the fifth, Sudalisun for the sixth, and Galiqugisun for the seventh. So although Wahketsi was the daughter of twelve moons, she was also one of the Seven Suns of the Cherokee!

Now she was worried that they would no longer be seven, and it would all be her fault. If only she didn't hesitate when she was supposed to kill the Ghost Spirit, Galiqugisun would not now be walking between the two worlds—the world of the living and the world of the dead. She had to hurry and get him back to the camp so she could use the herbs and roots she needed to stop his bleeding and remove the bullet in time to prepare the camp for a possible attack. The camp was just over a mile away from where the Cherokee people were being held. Even in the dark, under normal circumstances, she could make the walk in less than twenty minutes. But with Galiqugisun hindering her efforts, she knew that at least an hour would pass before she will feel the safety the camp would provide.

With all that was going on in her life at that moment—first, her best friend's life essence was pouring out of him and soaking her clothes, the blood was moving up her sleeve as if it was a living thing, second, she feared that her mistake may cause an attack on the camp and she had no way of warning the others, and third, and probably most important for her, she was still having, in spite of all that was happening, a difficult time reconciling her actions of the night with the feelings she was wrestling with inside herself. If it were not for these feelings, she kept telling herself, she wouldn't now be struggling to keep the presence of mind she needed in order to make a plan for a strategy that she hoped would save them on this night where, for the first time, everything she did went wrong. But she understood that plan she must for their survival, and so plan she did.

Once they finally made it back to the camp, she knew they had only a few hours before the sun would rise. All the braves of her war party wore their war face, and for most people, it would be near to impossible to distinguish one brave from another. But for Wahketsi, she could instantly recognize them. So the first thing she had to do was to stop the blood flowing from Galiqugisun's wound. While she was attempting to do that, she called Talisun and Tsoisun to her side.

These two were brothers, and they were excellent trackers. They could follow the slightest trail left by someone. A broken leaf, a stepped on twig that had been snapped in two, or the faintest ground impression would not go unnoticed by them. What they could gleam from what would go unnoticed by most people was almost unbelievable. Height, weight, sex, how many, and how long ago—they could determine all these things just by looking at a single footprint in the dirt. They worked so well together; it was almost as if they shared the same mind. Together, they both understood the ways of the deer and could run almost as swiftly as the deer. They could hide nearly in plain sight by remaining completely motionless for hours if need be.

"Talisun," Wahketsi began giving her instructions while she was operating on Galiqugisun's wound, "I want you to walk back down the blood trail leading here to our camp and erase all our tracks. Tsoisun, I want you to go ahead of Talisun. When you are far enough away from the camp, I want you to create another blood trail by changing our trail so that it leads away from camp."

They both would have to do this while working in darkness with only the light of the moon to guide them. For them, this would be no more difficult than it would be if the sun was shining on a bright clear day. The moon was back to being full in the night sky, and that was more than enough light for them to work with. There was only a few hours left before the sun would begin to make its appearance, so they would have to work fast.

Talisun would follow back down the trail leading into camp by covering over the disturbance of the dirt and blood along the way. He was to make sure to remove all indications of someone traveling that way, whether it was broken twigs or by wiping clean the blood from any leaves as he went back to the spot where Tsoisun would have changed the direction of the blood trail. Tsoisun would cut his own arm so his blood would create a new blood trail going in a direction away from the camp. Tsoisun's job was to lead the troops on a false blood trail, and then return back to camp later that evening after he stopped his bleeding and made sure he wasn't being followed.

Once Talisun reached the spot where the blood trail changed direction, he was to, first, create a second set of footprints to match Tsoisun's for a while so it would appear that two people went in the direction of the new blood trail. Then he was to walk backward making sure to step back into the footprints he already made until he was back to where he began. Then he was to hide himself under the grasses and leaves so he could be there in the morning to make sure the troops took the false trail.

While he was hidden, he was also supposed to observe how many troops were looking for them and what type of weapons and supplies they carried. Then he was to take that information back to Wahketsi. If he did not return to camp by noon, Wahketsi would have already prepared the camp to defend against the troops who showed up. It would be a last resort that she was hoping she wouldn't need, but she didn't feel she could risk moving Galiqugisun any further.

Even if somehow, Talisun failed to cover their tracks, the camp itself would still be difficult to discover. It was well hidden behind bushes that concealed its entrance. These bushes appeared to be growing out from the hillside, but they really covered a path that leads up the hill into an opening that couldn't be seen from ground level. Wahketsi chose this spot as their camp because this open area on the hillside had three natural caves they could use as shelter. Inside the caves, pools of water formed that was running down through the rock bed from the lake on top of the mountain. They collected their drinking water from the water running down the rocks, and they bathed in the pools formed by the running water. Wahketsi wanted to have one cave for herself. This way she could maintain her privacy. In spite of all her abilities, she was, after all, still a young woman. The others shared the other two caves.

Since the path was the only way into the camp, she told Nvgisun and Hisgisun to block the path with branches they would have to hurry and cut down from the forest. These two had a deep abiding reverence for the land and the forest. She chose them for this task because she knew that although they would use whatever measures that was necessary to block the path, they would also make sure to do as little harm to the forest as possible. Sudalisun, who did most of

THE PULL

the cooking for the group, and he was the one who prepared all the potions and medicines, was instructed to go gather up wood to build a fire. He would boil the leaves and blossoms of the stiff goldenrod plant, the stems from the shrubs of the witch hazel, and shavegrass so Wahketsi could use them to make a poultice to put on Galiqugisun's wound.

First, though, she had to remove the bullet that had struck his collar bone and fractured it. The bullet had ricochet off the bone and was now resting just below the surface of the skin in his upper back. She knew that this combination of plants and grasses she had chosen for Sudalisun to prepare would do three things. They would sterilize the wound, aid in stopping the bleeding, and help with the healing process.

Then Sudalisun would also boil the blue plant the Cherokee people had used to make medicine to heal the sick for as long as she could remember. Wahketsi thought about the first time she was given the blue medicine. She was just a little girl when all the children in the circle got sick with fever. The blue medicine man came and made all the children drink the blue medicine. In a few days, all the children were feeling better and back to running around and playing. Now she was hoping this blue medicine would help her friend avoid the fever during his recovery as well.

With Galiqugisun's life now out of danger, and she had sent two of her best trackers to prevent the soldiers from finding their camp, two of her other braves had made certain that the camp's entrance had been fortified, she felt, now, she could finally relax a little. Now the only way into their camp was on foot up the narrow path which would allow for them to defend a smaller area rather than getting stormed by men on horseback.

On the other side of the opening of their camp, the trail continued on up into the mountain. The next opening on the trail up the mountain is where they kept their horses. So if they did have to retreat, their horses would be available to them, but the soldiers' horses would be blocked from coming up the trail. She was still hoping that this plan that she had to conceive in haste would not be necessary, but she was satisfied that it would work if it should be needed.

Willa, the trails through the mountains had been traveled for hundreds of years by our people. Wahketsi knew them so well; she could travel for miles on this land that once all belonged to her people, but now was rapidly being taken away from them, and she would still know exactly where she was in relationship to the borders of the three states that made contact with each other: Tennessee, Georgia, and North Carolina.

Finally, after she had done all she could do to prevent her mistake from causing the life of her friend and bringing an attack on the camp, she realized how completely exhausted she was. With the light of the early morning sun just starting to creep into the entrance of her cave, Wahketsi decided she would allow herself to listen to the call of her body for rest and sleep. Sleep came without hesitation. It came so easily she had forgotten that she had laid Galiqugisun on the blanket in her cave because she needed the herbs she kept in there. She wasn't even aware that she had fallen asleep lying on the blanket right next to him. He had passed out almost as soon as he was placed on the blanket and the hot knife entered his pulsating wound.

CHAPTER 22

Vision of the Moon Goddess

While Wahketsi was asleep, the dream vision came to her for the first time. In the vision, she saw a round light as bright as the moon in the night sky come down from the heavens and land on the earth. Walking out of the ball of light was a woman who appeared to be the Moon Goddess. She was dressed in a long flowing garment that shimmered with white light as she moved. Around her waist was a sash that was knotted in the front and flowed toward the ground. It shone like it was made from the purest of silver.

Above her head was a garland made of twelve shining stars. Her long hair was black with two long pig tails coming down the front of her dress. In her left hand, she held what looked like a wand that curved almost into a circle at the top. It was silver in color. In her right hand, she had a rod that at the top of it were two solid stripes hanging from it. This one was gold in color.

At first, looking at the woman's face, for Wahketsi, was like looking at the sun at midday. When the woman began to move away from the ball of light, Wahketsi could begin to make out her facial features. The face that was coming toward her looked just like the face Wahketsi remembered her stepmother, Ahyoka, described when she spoke of Wahketsi's real mother, Wahetsi.

This woman was very beautiful, and her soft, smooth light-brown skin seemed to radiate with light. When she smiled, her teeth were as white as fresh milk poured into a bowl, and when she spoke, it was in a soothing harmonious melodic tone. It was heard inside Wahketsi's head. Even though the Moon Lady's lips were moving differently; Wahketsi could hear every word in her own tongue.

"Wahketsi, my beloved daughter!"

"Yes, Mother, I'm here!" This was the first time, in a very long time, that Wahketsi didn't remember feeling anger raging inside her. She had been angry for so long; she had forgotten what it felt like to be at peace with oneself. All she had ever known was that the pain in her heart never seemed to stop hurting.

"Mother, what is it that you wish of your daughter? All you have to do is say it, and I will do whatever you ask of me."

"You, Wahketsi, who is most beloved and treasured, I've come to take away the pain in your heart. I've come to bring the joy of womanhood to you my daughter. And I've come to show you what is to become of the people you love. Your people, whom you fight so hard to protect, oh, great and mighty warrior!

"But first, my love, you must put away your tools of war and be cleansed. You must not kill the Ghost Spirit. You must let him live so he can go back and tell his story of the innocent blood his people has shed on the earth. You must travel from this place. You must go and contemplate the holy rock and cleanse yourself in the holy waters! Then you must willingly suffer the agony of your people because of the blood you and your people have shed on the earth as well."

"Mother, these words you speak are hard to be understood. I don't understand."

"You will, my daughter, you will!"

"Mother, all my life I have loved your sister Ahyoka as my mother. She has been very good to me, and she has told me all about you, but it has been very hard for me to try to love the woman Mother Ahyoka described to me. I never got to know you, and I always wanted to know you for myself. I always wanted to love you for myself. I always wanted the pain of never getting the chance to know you, the pain of never being able to see you with my own eyes and love you with my own soul, to stop hurting my heart! But I could never stop this pain inside of me because I always felt it was my fault that you weren't here anymore. If I had never been born,

THE PULL

you would have lived, and Father would not have been so sad. I can't forgive myself for being the cause of your death and for bringing so much sorrow to Father's heart. He misses you even more than I do."

"My daughter, the time of my magic was fading away. The time of my life force of womanhood, where all creative magic comes from, my lovely little girl, was coming to an end. It was time for this magic to be reborn so the balance could be maintained. Restore balance, my child!"

Then the Moon Lady turned to walk back into the ball of light. Wahketsi began to feel the pain in her heart return and she yelled out, "Please, don't leave me alone again, Mother! Please! Stay with me! I have needed you in my life for so long. I have been angry for so long living without you in my life: All I have is pain in my heart when you're not with me! Mother! Please—stay!"

Wahketsi woke up in the cave still screaming for her mother. Then she realized that it had all been just a dream. When she realized that her mother was not with her, and that she was still all alone, she cried!

CHAPTER 23

Good Meets Evil

Early the next morning, the sergeant was the first to have his horse saddled and ready to go. There was a freezing chill to the morning air, almost like the coldness of death was accompanying it. The sun had not yet reached over the surrounding trees to start melting the dew off the ground. The pale, icy cold lifeless expressions on the faces of the dead men that were already being buried just a few feet away from where the horses were being kept seemed to mimic the white lifeless covering on the cold ground, making this early autumn morning seem even more eerie and strange.

While he was standing there waiting for the other men to show up, the events of the night before kept repeating themselves over and over in his head. The sound of laughter, her laughter, kept ringing in his ears. Why was the sound of her voice so penetrating, so piercing to his heart? Why didn't she kill him when she clearly had the chance? He found himself wondering a lot of things about her, like who was she? What did she look like under all that red paint? Would he ever see her again, and what would his response be when he finally does see her?

Will he shoot to kill first? What will happen to him the next time he hears her voice? Will he be so lucky again, or will she do what she was about to do the first time they met? He didn't know any of the answers to his questions; all he knew was that he couldn't stop thinking about her. He kept telling himself that all the answers lie with her. So even if it came down to a life-or-death situation, he promised himself he was going to see her again. But in order to do that, he had to first find her!

The three soldiers the captain said were the first sergeant's men were really men from the Georgia militia and were only wearing soldiers' uniforms because they had temporally join with the Army to help with the removal of the Cherokee Indians from the state of Georgia. These were the men that had been assigned to accompany him as his escorts from Camp Wool in Georgia to the camp near Rattlesnake Spring in Tennessee. They were chosen because they had already made several trips to the camps bringing Indians. Since the trip of taking the Indians to Tennessee was very dangerous, they were paid a dollar a head for every Cherokee they brought to the camps.

It wasn't smart to attempt to make this trip with more than thirty or so Indians at a time, and since the trip there and back took thirty days, sometimes longer, to complete, they would each be paid thirty dollars a month. There used to be more in their group, but the last time they made this trip, they were attacked by Indians, and these three barely escaped with their lives. While they were waiting for new men to be assigned to their group, they were promised fifty dollars each, almost two months' salary, if they got the sergeant to Rattlesnake. Once the sergeant reached Rattlesnake, the original plan was that the first sergeant would handpick his men to help him track down and kill the Death Raiders. But the night before, the captain made it clear, without saying as much, that he would not risk losing anymore of his own men.

So the first sergeant was being asked to go hunt down the most dangerous Indians in the Cherokee nation with men he didn't even know by their first name. No one even knew for sure just how many Death Raiders there were. He assumed, in order for them to move so swiftly and without detection, they had to be a small group. No more than possibly ten. But even if that number was correct, it still would mean that they would have more than a two-to-one advantage over his group. Not only were these Indians a perfect killing machine working together but they also knew and understood the forest and the mountain terrain far better than anyone going with him. When he considered everything that would be asked of his men, he knew they had little to no chance of surviving this mission, which meant that he also seriously doubted his own chances of surviving as well.

When the three men finally stood in front of the sergeant, he could see the fear in their eyes. They each looked like they were ready to go running and screaming into the woods to hide. If it wasn't for the fact that they were already too afraid to go into the woods, they just might have done that. In spite of the captain's orders, the sergeant felt he couldn't ask these men to go and die with him without talking to them man to man first. So he began by saying, "Men, I know that when you were assigned to escort me from New Echota to this camp. You didn't intend to be the ones who would be hunting down the Death Raiders with me. You were only chosen to bring me here because you had made this trip several times bringing Indians to these camps. But I want you to think about something.

"You got me here safe and sound and you three men have brought many Indians here and you have survived each time. There are not many men who can say they have traveled the roads you have and have lived through the type of attacks that you have. Only men of destiny survive the things you three have. I know you men know what happened here last night, and I know you know that some men didn't survive that attack last night. Those poor fellows over there who are now being put into the ground all died last night. But I didn't! Because I'm a man of destiny too!

"One of them Death Raiders came into my tent and I shot him. Before I shot him, I got a good look at him. What I saw was not a monster or a ghost but a man just like you and me. I can show you the blood to prove to you that they bleed just like we do. The first sergeant knew that he was taking advantage of how fortunate he was the night before. He couldn't bring himself to tell these men that the person he shot was a boy, no more than seventeen or eighteen years old. But he had to find some way to shake the fear from them if they had any hope of surviving.

"You are now soldiers in the United States Army, and when we signed our lives over to the government to serve this country, we did so voluntarily. As soldiers, it's not our job to question orders. Our job is to see to it that those orders get carried out. We may never have any say in what type of orders we are given, and we may not always like those orders either. But what we do have is a say in how we work together to carry out those orders. Men that stick together in battle can accomplish great things together. Men that trust each other and look out for each other have overcome many adversities together. If we can learn to do that, we will survive this mission. So we are going to track down these Dearth Raiders, and we are going to kill them because if we don't, then they are going to keep on killing until somebody stops them.

"On the way here, we only made a campfire during the day. We slept on the cold ground with only our blanket roll to keep us warm at night. We didn't do any talking among ourselves during the night for fear of bringing Indians to where we camped. So we didn't get the opportunity to get to know each other properly, but before we go, I want each one of you to tell me your name. Not just your last names. I don't want to call you by that anymore. I'm asking you to tell me your first name and a little about why you decided to joined the militia. I want us to become friends. We are going to have to become friends, not just an officer with his soldiers—friends!

"If we are going to ride into those woods, and if we hope to survive whatever we encounter in those woods, then we are going to have to trust each other. You men already know that my first name is Luke, and I was sent here to hunt down and kill the Dearth Raiders. That much you were told about me when you agreed to accept the assignment of bringing me here. But the mission to bring me here was put together in such a rush and with so much secrecy that I wasn't given much information about most of you. So why don't you go first?" The sergeant was pointing to the man that was standing the closes to him. He was a man of average height, and he looked to be around the same age as the sergeant, but he was wearing a wedding ring.

Now the first sergeant had just turned twenty-five, so he figured this fellow to be at least that old. His hair was dark brown and woolly. His sideburns, beard, and mustache covered most of his face like he hadn't shaved for weeks. His skin was tanned and rough from being exposed to the sun while working outside most of his life. He had a rugged mountain-man built. His hands were also rough and powerful looking, like they had taken a lot of abuse over the years in order to do the jobs that was required of them.

"My name is Paul, and I joined the militia so I could provide for my wife, son, and daughter. I was a farmhand most of my life, and I was promised if I joined the militia, I would receive land of my own. I wanted to finally be able to own some land where I could build a farm on it for my family. Now all I want to do is see my wife and children again."

"Don't worry, Paul, I can't promise you, but I will do everything in my power to see to it that you see your family again. How about you, what's your name?"

"I'm called Little John, sir, because of my father, who's called Big John." John looked to be no more than eighteen years old, and just by looking at him, the sergeant knew for sure that the person he shot the night before couldn't have been much older than the young man that was now standing in front of him. John had curly red hair, freckles on his face, and buck teeth, and he wore wire rimmed-framed glasses to help with his eyesight. He had a slender built, and his body didn't look like it had ever done any hard work a day in its life, nor did he look like he could endure the stress of physical labor. He was what you might call frail looking.

"My father is called Big John because he works for the lumber company. He goes out and chops down trees all day. He kept telling me that I don't have what it takes to be a lumberjack. I wanted to show him that I could be good for something, so I joined the militia so I could learn to shoot and fight the Indians. Now I'm a better shot than he is with the long riffle and with my pistol."

"Well, John, that's really good to know. We are going to need what you have learned, and I plan to put your skills to good use," the sergeant said. "Okay, let's hear your story, mister." The first sergeant was talking to the last man in the group. He spoke to him this way because he had already been told before he left Fort Wool that one of the men with him was a convicted criminal.

"Well, let me see. I think my name should be Matthew. That way we can call ourselves the four apostles and pray for a miracle!

'Cause that's what it's gonna take if you really think we are going to kill those Indians that came here last night.

"I only joined the militia to keep from going to jail, and there was nothing said about going on suicide missions hunting down Indians that can do what those Indians did. The idea is that you are supposed to be trying to avoid running into Indians, not to go looking for them. Especially not to go looking for those Indians that they call the Death Raiders! I think, after last night, it can safely be assumed that they're called Death Raiders for a very good reason!

"They came into this camp that had armed guards on duty. They killed them without one of the guards even so much as getting a single shot off. Do you understand that the only way something like that could have been done is for them to have killed all four guards at the same time? The two guards at the front of the camp were in sight of each other, and not only could the two guards at the back of the camp see each other but they could also see the two guards standing at the front of the camp.

"So these Indians were able to shoot all four guards by shooting arrows in the dark, mind you, at the same time so not one of the guards could cry out or give a warning. Then they even had the nerve to go into the officers' tents without waking a single one of them either and kill them too. You can give all the speeches you want, but if we do this thing, ain't none of us coming back. Not alive anyway!"

The first sergeant walked right over to the man called Matthew and looked straight into his eyes, because he was nearly as tall as the sergeant, and said, "Soldier, you still haven't told us about yourself."

"Okay, you want to know about me! I'm a gambler, a card cheat, and a horse thief. Oh, yeah, I'm also a ladies' man, but I have also been known to lie a lot." You could see that he was indeed the type of man that many women would swoon over. Even, maybe especially, in the uniform he was wearing, he looked like the type of man that could charm his way out of anything.

His hair was a slick, rich dark black, and he had dark eyebrows that were connected to each other in the center of his forehead. His mustache was trimmed and formed a goatee on his strong jawline and chin. He had a trimmed, fit built and his uniform fitted him perfectly. He was the type of man that could compete with most women when it came to keeping up his appearance. His movement was almost elegant or regal, and he exuded confidence in himself and in his abilities. He clearly was the oldest in the group. If he said he was thirty-six years old, you wouldn't be able to call him a liar. He didn't look like the type of man that had ever stuck his neck out for anyone else though. So the real miracle would be if he didn't take off the first chance he got!

"Okay, now that you have said your piece and made your point about what you think our chances are, let me make my point" was the Sergeant's reply while still looking the man called Matthew in the eyes.

"You are a convicted criminal. The only reason you're not behind bars is because you swore an oath to serve the state of Georgia and now this country. I'm sure you had your reasons for not wanting to go to jail, and I can only guess what those reasons were. But I don't think a man like you would do too well being locked up though. So I suppose you found some way to keep on talking until you were able to talk your way out of that one too!

"Where we're going, your smooth talking isn't going to be much help to us. So if you aren't going to be able to put those perceptive observational skills of yours to good use, then I suggest you try keeping your thoughts to yourself. Anyway, you missed a very important fact in your analysis of the events of last night. If these Indians really were so perfect in their ways of killing, I wouldn't still be alive now, would I?" The sergeant's face was now only a few inches away from the man called Matthew, and he was giving him a look that dared him to say another word.

"Look here, mister, we're going into those woods, and like it or not, you are coming with us. But the moment I even think you are going to go back on the promise you made to serve this country, or if you try to do anything to hinder this mission, I will shoot you myself. Have I made my point clear, soldier!"

"Well, Sergeant, that doesn't sound much like you're really trying to make friends, but yes, you made your point. And since you put it that way, I guess I will have to decide which is better—getting a bullet from a friend, such as yourself, or getting my head handed to me by one of those Indians.

"Oh, yeah, as far as you're still being alive and all, I'm still trying to figure that one out myself. But I can tell you this—there is something about your story that just doesn't add up. For one—"

"Well, soldier, why don't you just try to worry about us surviving this mission we have now and let me worry about how I survived last night."

"Yes, sir, Sergeant, I will try to do that!"

Now the man called Matthew said these words while mockingly giving the sergeant a salute. He felt that the only reason the first sergeant interrupted him was because he didn't want to discuss how he actually survive the attack the night before. Now to this man, Matthew, being the type of man that he was, this meant the sergeant was hiding something.

In spite of their instant dislike for each other, both men recognized the strength, determination, and will that each possessed. It was like looking at the two opposite sides of a coin. One had dedicated his life to being a man of integrity, honor, and discipline. He had used the skills, abilities, and opportunities life had given him to serve and help others. The other had dedicated his life to being an unscrupulous, fraudulent, and reckless man. He had used the skills, abilities, and opportunities life had given him to become shrewd and cunning so he could take advantage of others. These were the four men that were assigned the task of bringing an end to the reign of terror the Death Raiders had caused for almost two and a half years, and two of them would begin this mission hating each other.

Just then, the captain walked over to the sergeant. "At nine o'clock, we plan to have a service for the officers and the men that had to be buried this morning. I think it would help the morale of the men if y'all stayed until after the service is done. I couldn't help but listen in on some of what you had to say to your men. I was wondering, with you speaking all proper 'n like, if you wouldn't mind saying a few words over my friends before you go."

"Sir, the captain's orders were to leave at first light."

"I know what I said last night, but now I got a bunch of scared soldiers on my hand. I don't want them runn'n off somewhere out of fear of them dammed Death Raiders comin' back."

"Captain, I'm sorry, but I didn't really know your officers very well. I don't think it would be right for me to be the one to give some kind of eulogy over them."

"I don't need you to talk about them, you dang fool. I can do that on my own. What I need from you is to pick up my men's morale with all your fancy talking and words."

CHAPTER 24

Wahketsi Must Go to the Paint Rock

That morning, Talisun, who was now hidden so he could wait for the arrival of the troops, saw that there were only four soldiers following the blood trail left by Tsoisun. He became so excited that he had to resist the urge to take them out, one by one, himself. It was the shock of seeing that the blond little chief was still alive and leading the search party that changed his mind. There wasn't enough time, he remembered, to hear the story of what happened to Galiqugisun the night before because they had to hurry and cover their tracks to keep the troops from finding their camp. But now he wanted to know why this little chief was still alive! What does him being alive have to do with Galiqugisun getting shot?

When he got back to camp to make his report, the mixed emotions he was having showed on his face. He wanted to confront Wahketsi about the information he had, but the other three braves stopped him. They told him that Wahketsi had been screaming and yelling out in the cave all morning, and that they could hear her talking to her dead mother. Once Talisun heard everything that had happened, they all agreed that she was having a dream vision and that it would be very dangerous to disturb someone while they were in this trance. So they decided to wait until she came from the cave.

The sun was just now starting to set in the sky when Tsoisun showed up back in camp. The others had made a fire and were sitting in front of it. Nvgisun and Hisgisun had gathered wild potatoes and greens and were boiling them on the fire. Sudalisun was also roasting a duck. They all looked up when Tsoisun came to sit with them, and without saying a word, they all knew that he had successfully completed his mission. Just as they began to tell him the events of the day.

Wahketsi emerged from her cave. She sat down to the fire, and they all ate. No one dared to say anything before she did, so they all ate their meal in silence waiting for Wahketsi to speak.

When they were finish eating, Wahketsi began to tell them everything that had happened. She told them that Galiqugisun was doing fine. She had removed the bullet and his bleeding had stopped. Then she explained how he got shot.

"I was in the tent of the blond hair. My knife was at his throat, but I couldn't kill him. I didn't understand then why I hesitated. He woke up, and Galiqugisun must have heard the noise he made when he fell from his chair. He came into the tent, and instead of shooting me, the blond hair shot Galiqugisun. All the while I was bringing Galiqugisun back to the camp, I kept wondering why I hesitated in killing the blond hair. I felt it was my fault that Galiqugisun got shot, and I had to save his life or how could I ever forgive myself.

"When I finished healing his wound, I felt very sleepy, and before I knew it, I was in the dream vision. In the vision, I saw my mother, my real mother, and she spoke to me. She told me that I was not supposed to kill the blond hair. She said he has to live because he has a purpose for our people. Then she told me that I must travel to the holy rock and cleanse myself in the holy waters! Her words were very hard for me to understand, but she said she will explain everything to me if I do what she asks of me. When I woke up in the cave, that's when I realized that it wasn't real. That my mother was not with me, and that my real mother was still dead, and that it was all just a dream.

"Almost three years ago, when we first left the mountain circle, my father told me the story of the eagle and the owl. He also said that I would have a dream vision and that it would be very powerful. He said that I had to let the vision explain everything to me about that story he told me. I didn't believe him because I was so angry about our land being taken from us. Now with Galiqugisun badly hurt, the

THE PULL

Army soldiers looking for us, and our people still being forced off our land, I'm not sure what it is I should do."

This was the first time Wahketsi had ever shown any sign of weakness or confusion, and all the braves sitting around the fire knew that, for the first time in her life, she needed their help with making her decision.

They all understood how important it was for a person to obey the dream vision. The dream vision only came at a time when powerful messages were being sent from the gods to mankind. The person that was chosen to receive these visions was usually a powerful worker of magic and had the ability to explain the meaning of the words of the gods to mankind. They all knew that Wahketsi was this person and that she had to obey the gods.

The first to speak up was Tsoisun. "You should not worry about Galiqugisun. My brother and I can take care of him. I promise you that we will get him healthy and take him back to his family on the mountain."

Then Talisun said, "Since you were in your cave when I came back to make my report, I didn't get the chance to tell you that it's only four soldiers looking for us. I thought about taking care of them myself, but when I saw the blond hair, I knew I needed to wait to hear what you had to say about him. Now I know it was the will of the gods that kept me from killing him."

Then Nvgisun said, "Sowosun, you must not put saving our people ahead of the message from the gods. What if this message is the answer our people need to hear? Then you must leave us to get the answer so our people can understand why they are suffering right now. Besides, you leaving us is not such a strange thing for us to understand. We are used to it by now."

One week out of the month, Wahketsi would leave the braves while she went and spent time alone high up on the mountain where the lake was located so she could have water to bathe herself while she was away. This was what Nvgisun was talking about. He was hoping that by reminding her of this, it would make it easier for her to decide to leave them. He did manage to get a slight chuckle and smile from her because she appreciated what he was trying to do.

Then she asked, "What do you think the Moon Lady meant when she spoke of the Holy Rock and the Holy Water?" This question she asked revealed just how young they all really were. Hisgisun said, "Do you think she could be talking about the old painted rock where the hot water comes to the surface in the pools near there?"

Willa, for thousands of years, long before the first white man ever stepped foot on Cherokee land, the Cherokee people had known about the healing powers of the hot spring waters found just over the Tennessee border in North Carolina.

Our ancestors considered these waters to be holy because they brought all four elements together. They found the big rock and painted the secret message of the waters on the rock so all Cherokee people and other Indian people could be guided to the waters to learn the lessons of the true purpose and meaning of nature. It was a spiritual pilgrimage for our people to take. But this pilgrimage had not been taken for over a hundred years because the white man had brought wars to our land. This was where Wahketsi was to go to seek the answers to the story Chief Iahoo told her.

Sudalisun said, "That place is no longer safe for the Cherokee people. The pale faces have turned it into a place where they do business, and they charge people to come there so they can bathe in the healing waters. The trail to the Paint Rock is now used by farmers as a route to bring their livestock up from North Carolina into the Tennessee towns of Charleston and Augusta where they auction them off.

"Smoke now covers most of the Paint Rock from all the campfires that have been lighted at its base when these farmers would stop to spend the night at the rock. Most of the secret message on the Paint Rock is covered in black soot and can no longer be interpreted. This holy place, the rock, the grounds, and the pools of water have all been desecrated. It would be very foolish and dangerous to go there." Some agreed with Sudalisun, but the others felt she had to go there and that they should go with her to protect her.

While listening to all the comments about whether or not going to the paint rock was a good idea, Wahketsi remembered that her father talked about this place once. It was during a time when he was very sad. The time of the year had come when she was born. This time of the year always made her father sad because it was also the time of year that her mother died.

The last full moon of the month before was around the time of Wahketsi's birth. She was born at the time of the year when the sun and moon faced each other in the heavens. Creating the second time in the year when they are in perfect balance. This time of the year her people called the night of the year, and it was traditionally one of the times of the year that her people would have taken this pilgrimage to the Holy Rock and bathe themselves in the holy waters. When she was very young, her father only spoke once about this place to her, and she had forgotten his words, but now they were all coming back.

He told her that he loved her mother so much that once he had to risk his life just so he could marry her. He spoke about the time he went to the Paint Rock so he could become the man that would be worthy enough to marry her mother. He also told her that while he was making this pilgrimage, he found a cave in the mountains where there was a hot water pool that was away from where the pale faces bathe in the hot waters. Wahketsi thought to herself, *If I can only find that cave Father found, this pilgrimage may not be as dangerous as it now seems.*

After being quiet for several minutes, Wahketsi said, "It's decided. In the morning, I will leave for Paint Rock alone. Talisun and Tsoisun will remain here to look after Galiqugisun, and when he is well enough to travel, they will make sure he's returned back to his family on the mountain. Nvgisun, Hisgisun, and Sudalisun, you three will take care of the soldiers that are looking for us. Then you all must return to the mountain circle so you can be reunited with your families as well. Just remember that the blond hair is not to be killed.

"I'm going to go to the Paint Rock, and I'm not taking any of my weapons with me. I was told in the vision not to bring any tools of war to the holy waters. I'm leaving my rifle and my bow and arrows behind. I'm only taking my knife so I can use it to cut wood to make a fire and hunt with it so I can eat. Whatever the message is in the story my father told me, the answers to figuring out how to understand that message is at Paint Rock. So if it is the will of the gods that I must travel there, then I must trust them to guide me. I promise, when I return back to the mountain circle, when I see all you again, I will tell all of you everything I learned."

Willa, Wahketsi still didn't understand that when she left the holy waters, she would not be returning to her mountain circle.

CHAPTER 25

The Chess Match Begins

The sun was setting for the first sergeant and his men. It was still above the horizon, which meant that there was only a few hours of daylight left. They had been riding all day following the trail of blood that led away from their camp. The man Matthew rode up alongside the first sergeant's horse.

"The other two seem to be too afraid to say anything to you, so I guess I have to be the one to say something. We need to stop. We've been riding all day without taking a break. The horses are tired and they need to drink. It's going to be dark soon, and we don't want to be wondering around in these woods at night. We have to make camp!"

"Okay, Mr. Matthew, ride on up ahead and see if you can find a place for us to make camp. You can take the boy with you to be your lookout if you're too afraid to go alone."

"Don't you mean I have to take the boy with me just so you can be sure I'm coming back?"

"Okay, I just think it will be a good idea if you are never left alone. That way, I won't have to come looking for you, and I won't have to hunt you down before we find the Indians we are looking for."

"That's more like it, Sergeant. Honesty suits you! But you don't have to worry; I won't be trying to travel alone at night in these woods, so you can stop your worrying: For now!" The mental game of chess that started between these two back in camp was already starting to heat up, even though they were still just moving their pawns on the board searching for any weakness in their opponent's game.

"Oh, yeah, by the way, Sergeant, we won't have to find those Indians. They are going to be finding us soon enough! I already know that," Matthew said.

"You do?"

"Of course I do! This trail we've been following all day will not lead us to them. They are too smart to not have covered their tracks any better than this. They want us to go in this direction."

"Then why in the name of all that is holy in heaven are we following it? Do you have a death wish or something?"

"I already told you, Serge, it's not my intentions to die out here, and if that's your intention, then I will be justified in saving myself."

"Yes, I'm fully aware of your heroics in saving your own neck, Mr. Matthew. But since you said we need to make camp, don't you think you should be about the business of doing that?"

"Well, all right, but don't you forget you said I can take that sharp shooting kid with me!"

"I haven't forgotten, Mr. Matthew."

Willa, this is the way the first sergeant described his relationship with the man called Matthew to our people. He said it was always like a chess match between them. He said he wasn't much of a card player, but he considered himself a pretty good chess player. In the game of poker, the idea is to bluff your opponent into folding his hand, but with chess, the idea is to out think your opponent by anticipating his next move. He knew that the man called Matthew would try to divide up the group so he could get away. The first sergeant considered the young man John to be the one in the group to be most likely influenced by Mr. Matthew since his relationship with his own father wasn't a good one. Also, he kept calling him sir, even though he wasn't that much older than him. This meant to the sergeant that this young man wanted the approval of an older male figure.

So he decided that John would be his pawn in his strategy. While with the man Paul, the sergeant felt that since he had a family, he would take his responsibility more seriously. The obligation he felt to provide a home for his family would not be something he would take lightly. This was his dream to provide a home for them, and he didn't want to disappoint them. That's why Paul was his knight; he knew he would be willing to fight to keep his hopes of receiving land for his family alive. That day on the trail, when they were searching for Wahketsi, the first sergeant sacrificed his pawn so he could protect his knight.

Now with the man called Matthew, the first sergeant saw back at camp that he was a self-centered and cocky man and that he didn't love anything or anyone more then he loved himself. The first sergeant understood that when there is someone who is constantly challenging your every decision, it is usually being done out of fear or ignorance. Although, the man called Matthew used very convincing arguments to make his point, his sole motivation was fear and self-preservation. With a man like that, the first sergeant felt he had to try to take away the one thing he valued the most—this aura of invincibility he tried to project. So to the first sergeant, that was the man called Matthew's queen. In his heart, he truly believed he could convince others of his infallibility.

In order for him to win then, and keep the group together, he had to capture Mr. Matthew's heart. If he could only keep him focused on the possibility of an Indian attack, he wouldn't have to worry so much about him continually trying to challenge his authority. The man called Matthew asking for the young John to come with him was how the first sergeant maneuvered him into exposing his queen. With that move, he felt that maybe this man Matthew wasn't the confident man and expert gambler he presented himself to be. He certainly didn't appear to understand how the game of chess was played. This was the first weakness his opponent had revealed in his game, but for the first sergeant, it helped him to form his strategy on how he was going to keep the egotistical Matthew in check. Or so he thought!

So far, he had been successful in keeping the knowledge of Wahketsi from the captain and from his men. Only he knew that he was really searching for her, and he figured the only way to find her was to follow the trail they left for them because it was the only clue he had. Wahketsi was his queen, and protecting her existence was the key to his mission of finding her. He couldn't understand why the very thought of her was driving him to near insanity, but it was true; he was captivated by this woman who he could only recognize by her voice, having never even seen her actual face. All he knew was that what he felt the night before, in her presence, and what he felt when he heard her voice, was something he had never experienced before and he would never forget it.

Not too long after the man called Matthew and John rode away, a gunshot was heard. He and Paul hurried up to see if the other two were under attack, only to find out that the young John had killed a possum for their dinner.

"Now, Sergeant, don't be upset with the boy. I told him to go hunt us down something to eat," Matthew said.

"Mr. Matthew, that was very reckless on your part. That rifle shot could have been heard for miles."

"Yeah, but I figure, it really doesn't matter since you already said they know exactly where we are. Unless you're going to tell us why you're playing into their hands, why you think following a trail that has, most likely, led us into their trap makes any sense at all, I don't think having a hot meal is gonna change the situation we're already in very much, do you?" The man called Matthew had finally made his move to capture the sergeant's knight. He was trying to undermine the sergeant's decisions to pursue these Indians in the eyes of the other two men.

Now the first sergeant found himself being put back on the defensive again. He knew that the man called Matthew already had time to put doubt in the mind of his young pawn, and now he was attempting to capture his knight as well.

"So, Sergeant, are you going to tell us what's really going on? Why are we out here risking our necks instead of making a getaway, as fast as we can, toward the Georgia border? Don't give us that line about following orders either. That fat captain ain't ever seen a battle a day in his life. The only thing he has ever fought was the urge not to eat everything placed on the table. And just because his family

THE PULL

wanted to make sure nothing happened to their precious Bumpy by requesting you to come out here to take care of his Indian problem doesn't give him the right to order other men to their deaths. Don't get me wrong, I'm truly sorry about what happened to his friends. But they all knew what they were doing when they decided to follow their rich friend out here into this dangerous territory."

The first sergeant suddenly realized that he had woefully underestimated Mr. Matthew. Instead of having him in check, he had fallen for the bait, and now he was the one being checked. Not only was he about to lose his knight but now there was the possibility that his queen was also about to get exposed. The first sergeant was learning very quickly that the man called Matthew was, indeed, an excellent gambler and a pretty good chess player as well. And that he was extremely confident in his ability to win friends and influence people to see things his way.

Now if he didn't figure out a countermove soon, the man called Matthew's next move would have him in checkmate! If he should lose his knight this early in the game, the thought occurred to him, he may never find his queen. He hated that he had allowed himself to, once again, be placed in the situation where he needed to defend the orders to hunt for Wahketsi. But he realized that if he didn't respond to the man called Matthew's inquiry, he would have three deserters on his hands, not just one.

"Okay, let's make camp here and have something to eat, and then I will tell you what you want to hear, Mr. Matthew," the sergeant said.

They managed to set up camp and got a fire started just as the last rays of the sun were disappearing under the horizon. The young John had skinned and cleaned the possum and had it ready to be placed on the fire.

"Too bad we don't have some carrots, celery, onions, and some potatoes. I could've made a pot of possum stew instead of us just having to eat it off the bone like this."

Just as he finished speaking, young John noticed the expression on the first sergeant's face. "What's the matter, sir, you don't like possum stew?"

"I never actually had possum stew or possum for that matter. There are a lot of things I've had to eat since I've come here that I never considered being food before. During my time of traveling through the South, just to get to Georgia, I've had the opportunity to try many Southern dishes. It's amazing to me, all the different variations there is to cooking pork alone down here in the South.

"I enjoy a nice Christmas ham like anyone else, and occasionally having a pork chop dinner is nice. I even love having bacon with my eggs for breakfast, but chitlins, which I'm told are the intestines of a pig, hog head cheese, which I have to assume is made from the actual head of a hog, and let's not forget pickled pig feet. I think that one speaks for itself. I just never knew it was possible for someone to find a way to eat so many parts of one animal before I came to the South.

"If those examples aren't already amazing enough by themselves, I've also been offered to eat, in a stew or some other clever name for the dish, squirrel, rabbit, muskrat, and now, to my utter delight, I find that there is even a stew for possum. What I wouldn't give for a nice thick juicy T-bone steak with a baked potato with butter, sour cream, and chives right about now!"

"It sounds like the sergeant is starting to get homesick, fellas." The man called Matthew decided it was time for him to join the conversation. "What's the matter, Sergeant? You miss your mama's cooking? You miss getting all dressed up for dinner and eating off of that fine china? This is the South, Sergeant. Down here people just try to keep a roof over their heads and keep their family fed the best way they know how. Most of the folks down here don't have enough money to go out and buy enough steak to feed a household with eight, ten, or even more people living in it. You see, you could have grandparents, parents, children, and grandchildren all living under the same roof in the South. So people tend to eat what they can afford to raise, hunt, or trap."

"Fair enough, Mr. Matthew. Perhaps I should have been more considered. It wasn't my intentions to be insensitive to the struggles of the day-to-day life one has to face living under such rural country conditions. But what you really want to hear from me, I take it, is

THE PULL

why I'm down here pursuing these very dangerous Indians in the first place."

"Yeah, Sergeant, I think we all would like to hear that."

"Okay, since you men are also risking your lives to be here, I think I do owe you some type of explanation."

CHAPTER 26

The Makings of a Good Soldier

"Before I begin to explain why I'm here, I would first like to correct something you said, Mr. Matthew. For a soldier, following orders have nothing to do with the man that gave those orders. You seem to be under the assumption that because Captain Hastings is not a very likable person, this somehow gives you the right to disobey a direct order. It doesn't surprise me that someone like you would come to such a conclusion. I'm sure this is why you have spent most of your life running from the law. When a person has no respect for authority, he usually finds himself in trouble with authority.

"For a soldier, it is his duty to respect the chain of command. If he is unable to trust that this system of command has proven that it works, not only in time of war but also in peace time, then he is not worthy to wear the uniform. A true soldier puts his duty to his country before his life, Mr. Matthew. Now I know that is a concept that is foreign to you, so I don't expect for you to accept what I have to say. But if there weren't men who understood this one simple principal of war, then there wouldn't be any nations because no nation could stand for very long unless there were men who were willing to die in order to defend its right to exist. Now every soldier has his own story to tell as to why he decided to join the Army. If you listen carefully to these stories, somewhere in each of them lies the clue as to whether or not that man will make a good soldier or not. Men have come from all walks of life that have gone on to become great soldiers, and yes,

Mr. Matthew, I'm sure there have been gamblers and card cheats that have made very good soldiers as well.

"It's not what you do in life that determines what type of man you are. It's what you were born with when you came into the world that determines who you will become. What makes a good soldier, a good doctor, lawyer, or Indian chief, for that matter, is the one thing you lack, Mr. Matthew. Although, you have its opposite in abundance, you will never have the one ingredient it takes to be a good, honest man. That ingredient, Mr. Matthew, is character!

"That is not to say that you are not a character because you certainly are. But it is to say that the blood that pumps through your heart is only concerned about keeping you alive. It is impossible for your heart to care about another human being. There is no one you wouldn't swindle, cheat, or lie too, is it! I don't think that your own mother can trust you. Mr. Matthew, I do believe that you are evil personified!

"I also know that you are not a man that likes to hear the truth because even for someone like you, the truth still hurts. But you wanted this confrontation. You were asking for this showdown between us. You wanted to challenge my authority, and you wanted to try to divide up this group. You may have forgotten what I told you before we left camp, or maybe you didn't take me seriously. So let me say it again and for the last time. If you do anything to try to hinder this mission again, I will kill you!" the sergeant said.

"Boy, Sergeant, when you cut, you cut deep. You cut right to the bone, don't you! But since you think you know me so well, then you should already know that I'm not accustomed to having someone threaten my life and living. That is the second time you've done that, and the only reason you're still standing up right is because we're out here in this Indian Territory, and we still need each other right now to survive," Matthew said.

"You talk about me wanting to have a confrontation with you, but we haven't had our confrontation. No, not yet! Maybe where you come from a man can insult another man, and they have their confrontation with words like two women would do. But down here, where you are now, confrontation between two men only leaves one of them standing. So if you haven't already gotten us all killed, we are going to have our confrontation someday, I promise you that! But I'm sorry. Where are my manners? I interrupted your story. You said you were going to tell us the reasons why you came to these the woods in the first place. Please, continue!"

"Sure, with pleasure, Mr. Matthew, with pleasure." The first sergeant realized, perhaps a little too late, that all along the man called Matthew had been playing poker not chess. But was he bluffing when he threatened to kill the sergeant, or was he merely calling the sergeant's bluff? Either way, the first sergeant felt now was not the time to show weakness.

"My first response to the question you asked would be that I'm out here looking for these Indians instead of putting my tail between my legs and running like a coward would do because I'm following orders that were given to me by a superior officer. Regardless to what I may think of him as a person.

"Now, as for my second reason, I do have my own reasons for coming here. Back at camp, I told you men that I feel that I'm a man of destiny. It is this destiny that has brought me here. For a very long time, I've been having a reoccurring dream. In this dream, I hear someone calling my name. They sound like that are hurt and in a great deal of pain. They are calling to me to come help them, but their voice is so faint that I can barely hear them. In the dream, I get out of my bed and walk out of my bedroom. Then the voice becomes a little louder. I walk downstairs and out the front door of my house. Again, the voice gets a little louder. I start walking in the direction I think the voice is coming from, and I keep walking toward this voice until I realize that I have walked a great distant from my house. Then I wake up!

"I have always felt this dream was telling me that someone who lives far away from me would need my help someday. So when the request came for someone to go to Georgia to stop these Indians from killing the soldiers, I volunteered to come here. Because I believe this is what the dream was showing me."

"Sergeant, didn't you say that you felt that we, also, had a destiny to fulfill?" The man Paul, who seldom speaks at all, was the one asking this question. Perhaps he was only trying to keep the first sergeant and the man called Matthew from continuing to challenge each other to a duel. Or maybe he actually felt that he understood the meaning of the first sergeant's dream better than he did.

"Sergeant, future generations are going to read about what this act has done to the entire race of the Cherokee. And I have nightmares that they are going to condemn us for the things we have done to these people. You speak of following the orders of your superior officer, and that we are supposed to obey the chain of command. But you haven't seen nor have you witnessed personally some of the atrocities that have been done on this land that we are taking from its rightful owners. I was ordered by my superiors to shoot a father and his children simply because he refused to leave the land that his ancestors had lived on before him.

"I can only hope that my posterity, my children, my grandchildren, and even my great-grandchildren will understand that I was a private soldier executing the orders of my superiors and that I had no choice in the matter. Sergeant, in your dream, are you sure you got it right about who it was that was calling you to come save them?"

CHAPTER 27

The Pilgrimage

It was still dark when Wahketsi left her cave to make the walk up the trail to her horse. A screech owl, perched on a tree branch somewhere in the darkness where the horses were being kept, was piercing the night with its unsettling screams. In the distance, she could hear a wolf howling at the moon. Perhaps this wolf, she thought, had gotten separated from her pack and was hoping her mate would answer her calls and guide her home. Wahketsi felt, as she prepared to ride away from camp for the last time, she was now that lone she-wolf groping in the dark, wondering whether or not she would ever find her mate again.

Not knowing if she will ever even see her friends again, she felt that when they wake up and discover that she had already left, they would all be very sad. But she needed to leave while she still had the strength to do so. Leaving like this, without even saying goodbye, was the most difficult thing she has ever had to do. She couldn't help but feel like she was abandoning them. She knew this was for the best, but it still didn't change how she was feeling inside.

Everything in her life was changing so fast, she hardly had enough time to catch her breath from that most disturbing dream she had, and now, as a result of that dream, she was riding off all alone into pitch blackness and into the unknown. Although she knew exactly how to find the Paint Rock, and she was sure her horse would stay on the trail until the sun came up, she had no idea what she was going to encounter once she reached her destination. She simply didn't know what to expect, and this was creating a nervous tension that had her doubting her decision.

As she clung tightly onto her horse's bridle so she could throw herself onto it's back, she breathed deeply into her the chilled night air, and just as the cold air filled her lungs, her body started shivering once she was resting firmly on her horse's back. She wasn't sure if it was the chill in the air, or if it was the nervous tension that had her shaking so much. She decided that it was both the night air and the tension she was feeling working together to try to make her return to that warm fire she left burning in her cave to keep Galiqugisun warm while he continued to recover. He had just begun to slip in and out of consciousness, just long enough to take a few sips of water and to drink some of the blue medicine down. Leaving him in that condition was also causing her much pain and sorrow.

With the tears starting to well up in her eyes, she was determined to put some distance between her and this camp that she had called home for the last three years. Only space and distance would ease these feelings of sorrow and uncertainty she was having. Maybe if she just kept riding and not look back, she would feel better in time or, at least, that's what she was trying to convince herself to believe. That once she had traveled some miles away, everything that has happened the last few days would begin to make sense to her. And that the almost three years of her life she had just spent was not, somehow, all a mistake.

What did the Moon Lady mean anyway when she said she and her people must suffer for the blood they have shed on the earth? Wasn't she right to fight for her people and to defend their homeland? This was the land of her ancestors after all. Isn't a person, or even a people, justified in defending themselves from those who would kill them and take their heritage away? Why would they be blamed for killing those who were killing them? These were the strange words the Moon Lady spoke that were so hard for Wahketsi to understand. She knew that the holy people in her circle never went to war, and that the medicine people, also, never went to war; women and children didn't have to fight either. But she never thought that all should be excluded from defending their land.

She started to remember her father's words that day he spoke at the first meeting at Red Clay when he said that the gods were no longer happy with the Cherokee people because they left them to serve the gods of war. All her life, her people had been at war with the white man, and she had never known a time when there wasn't war. So she never knew of these other gods and their other way of life. Could it be that, somehow, there is never a justification for the taking of human life and the shedding of human blood? But how could something like that be true? How could her way of thinking, and the way all people thought for that matter, be so wrong? Is this the path, or the teaching, that was the reason why her father refused to fight to protect their land from being taken away from them? Are these gods he spoke of the ones that led him onto this path?

Willa, these are the thoughts that were on Wahketsi's mind as she rode away from her camp that early morning before the sun was up. She kept on trying to figure these very hard questions out until she decided that she didn't know the true answers. Now she was beginning to doubt everything she had always thought to be right. Finally, she had to admit to herself, that she needed to understand the meaning of the story her father told her of the eagle and the owl. She promised herself that this time she would really try to figure out its meaning once she reached the holy rock.

After a few hours of riding in the dark, she saw the first rays of the sun begin to slowly chase after the darkness, causing it to eventually flee away. She knew that the braves she left sleeping in their caves would soon be awakened by the warmth of the sun's energy. Soon after that, they will become aware of the fact that she had already left. And she knew they would all be puzzled as to why she left without saying goodbye. This made her anxiety return, and she had to refocus on her mission.

She couldn't help but wonder what they would think of her for this very difficult choice she had to make. She kept hoping that as they planned their dangerous mission for today, they wouldn't let her absence become a distraction. This time they won't have the element of surprise. These soldiers that are hunting for them would be expecting an attack, and they will be ready to fight for their lives.

THE PULL

She didn't want them to be worrying about her now but to focus on the mission at hand. This, however, didn't mean that she wouldn't be worrying about them all day.

Willa, Wahketsi was right. When the other braves discovered that she had left during the night, they all became very sad. They mourned for Wahketsi as if they had lost her in battle. They couldn't understand why she felt she had to leave without saying goodbye and not giving them a chance to see her off. It was Galiqugisun, who had finally awakened, that spoke up. They all looked to him for leadership whenever Wahketsi was away.

Still being very weak and lying motionless on the blanket in Wahketsi's cave, he first listened to everything that was told to him. He felt that even though he had only just heard everything that happened while he was passed out recovering from his gunshot wound, he needed to speak so that his words could console his friends.

"We must not allow ourselves to be sad for Wahketsi. If what you all have told me is true, then the gods have chosen her to deliver their message to our people. It could not have been easy for her to leave us. We all must believe that. If she would have waited until morning to leave, she wouldn't have had the strength to go, nor would we have been able to allow her leave us. She did the only thing she could have done to make sure she didn't refuse the gods' request for her to come to them at the Paint Rock. Now she would want us to remember what she told us to do. She would expect us to be brave and carry out our mission. I'm only sorry that I can't go with you to help keep the soldiers from finding our camp and from following after Wahketsi.

"I would like to change one thing she said though. I don't think Talisun and Tsoisun need to stay here with me. I would feel better if I knew that all of you were out there together protecting her from the soldiers by making sure they don't even have a chance to pick up her trail."

Willa, even now, after all that happened in the tent that night, Galiqugisun was still more concerned for Wahketsi's safety than he was for his own life.

"You don't have to worry about me. I'm sure it will be all right for me to spend the day alone here as long as I have drinking water. I think I will even try to eat a little something too! Just make sure to leave everything close to my right side. It doesn't hurt too much to move my right arm."

CHAPTER 28

A Planned Attack

"I want all of you to go to carry out this attack. This way, you all will be stronger, and you will be able to mount a powerful attack. If you charge them in force before they have time to make a defense, they will panic and they will run first to find safety. Once you have them on the run, you must separate them from the blond hair.

"He must not be harmed because this is the will of the gods. You must do this without allowing him the chance to reach his rifle so he will not harm any of you. They all must not have time to draw their guns. You must stay behind them so they will not be able to take aim with their guns but only have time to concentrate on fleeing. This means that your charge must be swift and it must be precise. Once the blond hair is separated from the group, then you must separate the other soldiers from each other so that they're all running in different directions away from each other. Just make sure that no one is chased in the direction of the Paint Rock.

"Talisun and Tsoisun, you two should take care of the blond hair. Once you have him far enough away from the others, you must separate him from his horse. He should be chased back in the direction they came from. This way, his only choice will be to walk back to his camp. Make sure you leave him with water to drink. He should be able to make it back to his camp before nightfall. For the other three soldiers, each one of you will pick one of them. After you have chased your soldier far enough away, it will be up to each of you to determine how he will die.

"Now the trail Tsoisun had led the soldiers on through the woods would eventually come out into a wide open meadow that was nearly a mile wide before the tree line of the forest picked back up on the other side. About halfway between the two forests, there was a creek that came from a spring that ran down from the mountain lake. Any other morning, this would be a beautiful, picturesque scene to behold—the field of green grass with its autumn patches of yellow, orange, and brown shades of grass meandering through it".

In this high mountainous terrain, the sun seems to be moving at a very leisurely pace. It just took its time moving over the hills and valleys in the early morning. So the fog from the night before was still making a thin layer of haze hover just a few feet above the field in places where the sun hadn't reached yet, and the sparkling clear spring water running over the rocks in the creek bed was still frosty cold but not frozen.

Yes, Willa, any other morning this would have been a beautiful scene to behold. But this morning, it would be the scene of a very violent attack on animal and man. Knowing that the soldiers would have to follow the trail out into the meadow, the young Suns of the Cherokee had no problem picking up their trail and quietly followed them until they reached the opening. They waited for the soldiers to leave the cover of the forest and entered out into the meadow. Once the soldiers were clear of the forest, a single arrow was fired. This arrow hit the first sergeant's horse high on the fatty tissue of its right thigh. Then the braves, all at once and without warning, began shouting their battle cries while firing their rifles; they charged the soldiers that were now out in the opening with no place to take cover.

The soldiers, being completely caught by surprise, all took off toward the tree line in the distance. The first sergeant's horse, however, came up lame and could not gallop at full speed. He had no choice but to try to make it back to the forest they just came from. He veered off from the group seeking cover from the nearest trees he could find. It was Talisun who chased the first sergeant toward Tsoisun, who had stayed back in the shadow of the trees so he could be the one to fire the arrow that struck the first sergeant's horse. Using the trees for cover, he swiftly ran on an angle to the first sergeant's horse, so he could time just when the first sergeant's horse reached the trees.

Meanwhile, the other three soldiers were racing desperately for the tree line in the distance so they could take cover. When they reached the creek, two of the horses took the creek in a full gallop, but the young John's horse decided to try to clear the creek in one leap. The jump was missed, and the horse landed just below the creek bank, causing it to tumble forward, instantly breaking its neck. When this happened, John was flung from his horse and landed unconscious off to the side in the grass.

He would later wish that he would have died with his horse that day. The other two men didn't even see what happened to John. Maybe they caught a glimpse out of the corner of their eyes, but they certainly didn't have time to make any sense out of what had just happened, nor were they in any position to offer aide to their fallen friend.

Was it the instinct of knowing their fate, or was it just poor judgment on their part? It could have just simply been caused by the fear of the moment, whatever it was. The two men got separated from each other before they reached the trees. Had they stayed together, there may have been a slim chance they could have defended themselves, but once they separated that chance was no more. Paul's horse was very fast, and he began to pull away from the man called Matthew's horse once they had a clear stretch of field before them. The man called Matthew managed to look back in time to see two of the Indians veer toward the fast horse, and he decided that he didn't want to continue in the same direction. This left only one Indian chasing after him. He, being the type of man that he was, thought that his situation was now better than that of Paul's.

The sun was almost blinding as the first sergeant's horse was struggling to get back to, what he thought, would be the safety of the trees. The light was so bright on his eyes that he couldn't see anything past a few feet into the woods, so he didn't see Tsoisun tracking him from the forest. His only thought was that if he could only get to the cover of the trees, he would at least have a chance to mount a defense for his life. But his horse was beginning to have a severe hobble, and he couldn't understand why the horse of the Indian that was chasing him hadn't overtaken him yet. No matter, he had finally made it back to the cover the trees would provide for him; this was the last clear thought he remembered having.

As soon as the first sergeant entered back into the forest, and before his eyes even had time to fully adjust from the bright light of the sun, Tsoisun, running at full speed, leap from the ground onto the back of the first sergeant's horse, knocking him off. Tsoisun fell on top of the sergeant and held him down until Talisun, whose horse was now galloping at full speed, jumped from his horse even before it came to a full stop and struck the first sergeant across the head with his club, rendering him unconscious.

It was the throbbing in his head that force consciousness to return to the first sergeant. His blurred vision was slowly beginning to clear up, but the memory of the events earlier was returning even slower. He laid there on the ground too afraid to move a single muscle. He was trying to figure out if he was dead or alive, and if he wasn't dead, then why not? It was the sensations of the pain in his head and the ringing in his ears that proved to him that he was, indeed, alive. But why was he still alive? That's the one thing that didn't make any sense.

It was all starting to come back. The very sudden attack that happened when they were in the field, and then the other soldiers fleeing in the direction of the distant forest. His horse being injured and his desperate attempt to flee for cover were all coming back now. He remembered that just at the moment he thought he would be able to get his riffle so he could take a defensive position behind the trees, he was knocked to the ground, and then everything went black.

Yeah, that's right, my horse was hurt! He sat up looking for his horse only to feel his head spinning like a top. Placing both hands on the ground to steady himself, he forced his eyes to focus. That's when he discovered that his horse was nowhere in sight. His rifle, saddlebag, blanket roll, and his canteen of water were all there, but not his

THE PULL

horse. Seeing all his belongings on the ground made him realize that someone took the time to leave all his stuff but took his horse away.

This meant that they wanted him alive but not able to travel very far. Why was keeping him alive so important? Then he remembered the other soldiers, and he wondered what fate had befallen them. Were they out there somewhere stripped of their horse as well? He slowly stood to his feet so he could look out over the field to see if he could see any of his friends. He thought he saw a dead horse lying on the ground in the far distance. He didn't think it best to make the walk out into the open field just to confirm whether or not it was a horse of one of his soldiers. He didn't see anyone else anyway, and he didn't want to be exposed out in the open field again.

Next, he thought, with the sun being directly overhead, it had to be around noonday. If he started walking now, he could make it back to camp by the time of the evening meal. It was only yesterday morning that they left camp, and the captain's warning to not return back to camp unless he had killed the Death Raiders was already starting to echo in his head.

He couldn't return to camp so soon after leaving. He couldn't return to camp without his men only one day after they left, and he couldn't return walking on foot without even having a horse. How could he explain what happened? How could he explain that he knowingly led his men into an ambush? He didn't mean for things to turn out this way, or at least he was hoping for a better outcome then this. But, yes! It was his fault that they got attacked the way they did. He knew that he was following the trail that was left for them, but he was hoping the trail would lead him to her.

He knew that he was responsible for the lives of the three men that rode into these woods with him, and now they may all be dead. If only he could understand this feeling that was driving him to find her. If he could have just cleared his head long enough to have made a different decision, maybe they would still be alive. Why these Indians didn't just kill him too! Why did they leave him alive to suffer and agonize over the choices he's made recently?

He told himself, I'm a trained officer! *I graduated at the top of my class. I come from a long line of military men. My father is a captain in the Army, my grandfather was a general, and his father before him was also a general. How could I have failed so miserably on my first real mission?* He thought about how proud his family was when he decided to continue the family tradition by joining the Army. *But would they be proud of me now? Would they condone my actions that have left me without my men and standing all alone in the forest? Or would they feel what I'm feeling now! Would they feel that I have disgraced the family's name too!*

"Everything I've done, from lying to the captain about what happened in my tent, to threatening Mr. Matthew, to leading my men into this ambush, it all has been because I wanted to see her again. I just don't seem to be able to stop being drawn to her. It's almost as if I'm being uncontrollably pulled toward her, and I have no power or strength of will to prevent it from happening to me!

"From the moment I saw her, I have not conducted myself like a trained soldier, nor has my mind functioned like it has been honed by generations of military conditioning, teachings, and traditions. My recent actions haven't been responsible at all, and this behavior is not something I'm accustomed to. In fact, I don't feel I can even recognize the man that I've become lately. It's as if I'm under some kind of spell or something. What has she done to me?"

Now as he stood there considering his next move, he realized that there were only two choices he could make. He could walk in the one direction that leads to safety and life, but he would have to face certain humiliation and shame, or he could walk in any other direction and face the unknown and probably death. Only one of these choices, however, held out the possibility of finding her. So he decided he would rather face death if it meant there was a probability of seeing her again than to live with the knowledge that he will never see her again.

But how was he going to find her? He knew nothing of this land and even less of the woods where he found himself. He knew that if he took the direction back the way they came, it would lead to the camp, but what direction would lead him to Wahketsi? Just then, he saw a strange sight. A white deer, which seem to have come out of nowhere, was walking along the edge of the creek. This deer was so white, it was almost bright white, like the first snow of the year always appears to be. It was walking along the edge of the creek and following its path back up into the mountain from which it flowed.

Willa, for reasons he said he never quite understood, the first sergeant felt that he was supposed to follow that deer. So he quickly gathered up his things and hurried toward the deer that was all the way across the field. He, however, would stay within the tree line so he wouldn't be exposed. This way he would reach the creek a little after the deer had already started up the mountain.

CHAPTER 29

Where Their Paths Crossed

It was now midday, and Wahketsi had been riding all morning. She needed to stop and give her horse a rest and a drink since she had only stopped that once to let her horse drink at the mountain creek that she had to cross several miles back early that morning. This stop, however, was one of the watering pools that dotted the trails through the mountains. She wasn't certain if the water gathered in these pools naturally, or if some time in the distant past her people made sure there would always be water on the trails by digging down deep enough into the earth to bring the water to the surface. Either way, she needed to rest, and she and her horse both could use the drink.

After she found a nice comfortable place near the pool, but well hidden from the trail, she undid the knot tied across her chest from the rolled up blanket that she was caring on her back. Before she left her cave that morning, she placed all the things she would need to take with her in a blanket that had been first folded in half and then rolled from one corner to the opposite corner so that everything would remain inside and then the two ends could be tied to make a backpack.

In her blanket was a small metal pot that had a handle that hooked on both sides of its top, a flat metal pan, two wooden bowls of different sizes, a wooden cup for drinking, and a wooden spoon. She had a deerskin bag of ground-up corn and a bag of dried smoked deer meat. There was also a pouch that had a flint rock in it so she could make fire. She also had one change of clothes. She kept her knife in a holster around her waist and her deerskin water bag tied on a string hanging over her shoulder.

Now that her horse was watered and was grazing on the grasses and shrubs, she could take this time to get a little rest herself. She sat with her back settled up against a tree and began chewing on the dried pieces of deer meat from her bag. For some strange reason, she found herself thinking about the Ghost Spirit. She didn't understand why he kept coming to her mind. She only knew that she still felt something very strange whenever she thought of him. She even caught herself worrying that he may have gotten hurt during the attack planned for early that morning.

She asked herself, *What is this thing that makes me think about him so much? Why do I feel this way that I do? I'm a proud Cherokee warrior, and the daughter of the chief of the mountain people. Like my mother before me and her mother before her, my responsibility is to see to the care of my people. Are not these feelings I'm having for him somehow betraying my people? But why does my body want so badly to be close to his body? What type of magic is this? Has this Ghost Spirit placed me under some kind of spell?*

After falling asleep for a few hours, Wahketsi was awakened when a crow called out as it flew over her head. She was tired from not getting enough sleep the night before, but she decided that it was time to continue on her pilgrimage to the Paint Rock. Now having more questions than answers, she was determined to reach the holy rock as soon as possible. She decided that if she rode on all through the rest of the day and all through the night, she would reach the holy grounds where the hot water pools were located a little before sunrise. Then there would only be a matter of a few short miles to go before she would be standing on the bank of the river in front of the rock itself.

With her horse watered and fed from grazing, and her now feeling well rested and having her thirst quenched from filling her water bag and her hunger satisfied from eating the smoked deer meat, she rolled her things back up in her blanket and tied the blanket once again in a knot between her breasts. Then she decided that she would walk on foot for a while so her horse would have a little more time to rest since she knew she would be riding her all through the night. Besides, her leg muscles were still a little sore from riding her horse with only a blanket on its back to protect her inner thighs from the constant friction caused by the motion of her horse's shoulder blades. *This walk will do us both some good*, she reassured her horse and herself.

The first sergeant had been following the course of the creek as it twisted and winded its way back up the mountain. He would only occasionally get a glimpse of the white deer as he continued to pursue it up the mountain side. All day he forged ahead through the water and mud until he lost track of time. Finally, as the day was beginning to turn into evening, and he was becoming exhausted from the non-stop strain he was placing on his body, he came across the mountain trail that intersected with the course of the creek that he had been following all day. It was there, at this intersection, that he saw a single set of horse hoofprints in the mud as it crossed the creek. Later, when he told this story to our people, he would say that we don't ask him how he knew that those hoofprints belonged to Wahketsi's horse. He just knew that they did!

He immediately searched for the white deer. Maybe he wanted to somehow express his gratitude to this wild animal or something—he wasn't sure why this urge came over him, but there was no sign of the deer to be found. Just as the white deer seem to have appeared out of nowhere, it seemed to have disappeared the same way. The first sergeant, now realizing that it would be dark soon, decided that he would have to make camp there tonight. He figured that he would just have to pick up Wahketsi's trail first thing in the morning.

For now, he needed to find a safe place he could roll out his blanket so he could get some sleep. He had been walking up the side of the mountain all day and didn't even stop once to rest or to eat. Now he was feeling just how tired his body really was and just how much he needed to get something to eat. His stomach was complaining to him about going all day without being fed. He managed to find enough space behind a boulder-sized rock that would hide him

THE PULL

from the trail. He figured, all things considered, this is as about a safe of a place as I'm going to find out here.

Once he had his blanket unrolled behind the boulder, he decided that it was then time to solve his hunger problem. Remembering that there should be some Army-ration-issued packets of beef jerky in his saddlebag that he had flung over his shoulder and had been caring around with him all day, he decided that the beef jerky would have to suffice as his meal for the day. He thought, *I will just have to wait until morning to hunt for some fresh meat.*

As he sat on his blanket with his back resting against the boulder while pulling on the beef jerky with his teeth, he couldn't believe how happy he was feeling about finding those horse tracks in the mud. He could only describe what he was feeling as elation. He knew that those tracks would lead him to her, and that everything he had done, for good or for bad, didn't even seem to matter anymore. The only thing that mattered to him now was he was sure for the first time since he left camp that he was going to find her!

CHAPTER 30

The Paint Rock and the Moon Lady

It was still very early in the morning when Wahketsi approached the Paint Rock on horseback, and except for a few squirrels busily running from one tree to another, the trail was deserted of all other life. She sat on her horse staring at what once was the pride of her people. The barely visible markings on this rock summed up the collective knowledge of generations of her people going back for thousands of years. Now that knowledge, like her people, was about to fade into obscurity. Looking at the red painted symbols that were still visible enough to make out, she could see the figures of people.

There were also drawings that looked like birds and others of what appeared to be fish. Then there were drawings of four foot animals, maybe they were wild hogs or maybe even the buffalo, that a long time ago could be seen by the tens of thousands gracing in the plains once you cross over the mountains. She wasn't sure which it was, only that nothing was clear about the drawings she was staring at.

Wahketsi didn't understand what it was she was looking for. She understood that the red paint was the color that signified that the paintings on the rock were done by those who were considered to be holy among her people. Her mother was of the holy people, which meant that by birthright, she was also among the holy people. But she never felt that she truly belong among them because her mother was never there to teach her the ways of the holy people and the magic they could make. Now she felt it was unfair to expect her to understand things she had never learned.

Oh, what am I doing here? How are these drawing supposed to make any sense to me? I can't even see most of the drawings to even know what they are supposed to represent anymore. Why was I chosen to come here when I have turned away from holy things and became a warrior instead? Looking down at her hands, she thought, *These are not the hands of a holy one. These hands are stained with blood!*

Willa, just as Wahketsi was turning her horse away from the rock in frustration, she happened to look across the river. Standing on the bank on the other side of the river was a woman that appeared to be the Moon Lady from the dream vision. She was motioning with her hand for Wahketsi to come to her. Wahketsi became petrified with fear, and she couldn't move. How can the Moon Lady from my dream be standing on the bank of the river while I'm awake?

Then all of a sudden, and without any command from her, Wahketsi's horse started wading into the water of the river. As the icy cold water slowly started to rise up her legs until it was nearly waist high, she was still unable to look away from the lady standing on the bank. Her mind was trying desperately to give her body a command that it would understand, but her brain was unable to formulate a single coherent thought.

Finally, her horse walked out of the water and up the bank to stop in front of the lady that seemed to have summoned it as if by magic. The lady held out her hand to Wahketsi's horse, and when she opened it, there was a red apple in it. Her horse accepted the apple as if it understood that this was its reward for being obedient. "Oh my, what a magnificent animal, and she tells me that her name is Black Mist because she travels silently through the night," the Moon Lady said.

Wahketsi was still staring at the lady. Only her clothes were different—she was no longer wearing the long flowing garment but was now wearing a white buck skin dress that had embroidery of the sun, moon, and stars going around its collar on the end of its sleeves and around the hem of the dress. The dress came down below the knees, and she had white buck skin boots that also had the matching embroidery at their top.

Except for the fact that she was not shining with light, this woman looked exactly like the Moon Lady of the dream vision. This meant, to Wahketsi, that this lady also looked exactly like what she remembered being told her mother looked like. It was one thing for Wahketsi to dream of seeing her dead mother alive, but it was beyond her understanding to be awake and see someone who looked exactly like her mother. The events of the last few moments were just too incomprehensible for her mind to grasp!

"Oh no, my child, you are all wet! Please come down! We mustn't let you become sick. We have much to do, and there is much for you to learn." Wahketsi heard the words the woman spoke to her. They registered somewhere within her consciousness, but she was still unable to process the information her senses were, all at once, bombarding her mind with. So her body was still not receiving instructions from her brain.

The lady reached up and helped Wahketsi down from her horse. She walked her over to where she already had a fire burning. She undid Wahketsi's backpack and then removed her wet clothes. After she dried Wahketsi's shivering body, she covered her with a blanket that was made from bear fur, and Wahketsi's body, being smothered in the warmth, immediately stopped shaking.

Then the Moon Lady sat her down in front of the warm fire. She had warm pumpkin soup, hot flat bread made from yellow corn, cooked mashed green pea spread seasoned with salt and cucumber juice, and blackberry tea for Wahketsi to eat and drink. Once the aroma of the hot bowl of soup and the flat bread that was placed in front of her, it started to activate Wahketsi's taste buds, causing her mouth to salivate; she slowly began to revive from her momentary trance.

The hunger pangs of not eating since the day before caused her motor skills to also slowly return. Before she even realized it, she found her hand dipping some of the flat bread into the pumpkin soup and raising it to her mouth. Next, she was spreading the green pea spread on the bread and poured herself a cup of the blackberry tea. As she poured the tea, she noticed how the sunlight made the tea change in shades from blue, purple, and violet as it filled her cup. Drinking down the hot blackberry tea brought a nice warm feeling to her tummy. The whole time she was eating, she couldn't take her eyes off of the woman that was setting across the fire from her.

Finally, after waiting to make sure Wahketsi had enough to eat, the woman spoke. "I've been waiting for you to come to me, my child. The conditions on the earth have made it necessary for us to visit your people again. We are the Old Ones. We are the First Ones!"

"Why do you look like my mother?" Wahketsi interrupted. "Are you my mother?" Wahketsi asked this question, not even sure if she really wanted to hear the answer.

"I'm the mother of all living, so yes, my child. I'm your mother!"

"But how can you be my mother when my mother is dead?"

"Your mother lives in me, just as I live in you, and we are one!"

"I don't understand! You speak words that are hard to understand."

"Wahketsi, my lovely little girl, everything is not for you to understand. Understand this, and please trust in this. You have been chosen to know all the things that must come to past for your people. But the understanding of why these things have to take place on the earth has not been given for you to know. A child that comes from you who will live in the future will know these things. So the understanding is for those who live in the time of fire. That time is yet in the future.

"You have come here to understand the meaning of the story your father told you. Ever since you heard this story, you have struggled with trying to interpret its meaning, and even though you can't seem to understand the importance of this story, you haven't been able to stop thinking about it. Is this correct?"

"Yes, I can't get that story out of my head. I want to know what it means, but I don't know how I'm supposed to understand this story when I don't know what I'm supposed to be looking for. I came here to the Paint Rock because I was told that it would reveal the secret message of the story to me." When Wahketsi said this, she looked at the woman as if she was expecting her to acknowledge that she was the one who sent her to the Paint Rock. But the only acknowledgement that came was a sparkling in the woman's eyes. "Yet there is nothing that I can clearly understand on this rock either," Wahketsi exclaim!

"Daughter, the message that is contained on the Paint Rock was placed there for those who already knew what it was they were seeking. So only those who already knew the secret could understand the message. But the location of where the message was to be place was chosen so those who didn't know the secret could, through contemplation and careful observation, still come to understand the message the rock contained. The message is the message of life! Life, my child, and how it must be maintained is what the message on the Paint Rock once explained to all those who came to this holy place!

"Look across the river at the Paint Rock and tell me what do you see?"

"I see the rock."

"Yes, but what do you see below it?"

"I see the water of the river."

"That's right, and what do you see above it?"

"I see the sky above it."

"That's also right! So just by taking the time to notice the location of where the rock sits, you have made a discovery."

"I have? What have I discovered?"

"My child, you have discovered the three elements needed for life: earth, water, and air!

"The message was placed here on this rock, at this location, because this location reveals the meaning of the message. Now do you understand why we are here?"

"A little, but I still don't understand the story of the eagle and the owl."

"In time, my child, in time. Now you must get dressed. In a little while farmers will be stopping at the Paint Rock for the night on their way to take their livestock to market. We will observe how the meaning of the message on the rock unfolds." Wahketsi hurried to dress herself in the change of clothes she brought with her while her wet clothes were still drying by the fire. "How can we be here when the pale faces come? Won't they see us?" she asked.

"Don't worry, they won't pay any attention to us. They won't even notice your horse or our fire."

Wahketsi wondered, *What kind of magic can make the eyes not see what is there?* She wanted to ask her mother—Wahketsi decided that these words felt good to say and she like hearing them come out of her mouth—how come the farmers won't be able to see us? Just as she finally found the courage to ask the question, she heard the noise of the horses and cattle coming up the trail. It turned out that it was only three men: an older man and two younger men who appeared to be his sons. They were driving their cattle to the market. It was a small herd of about twelve beef cows and seven little calves that could be used to make veal meat.

"Come, daughter, let's watch how the cows feed themselves." Once the farmers stop at the rock, the cows all began to pull up grass and shrubs from the ground and began chewing. Once they finished eating, they went to the river's edge to drink water. Then the calves drank the milk from their mother's udders.

The woman asked, "Do you see, my daughter? Now are you beginning to understand?"

"Yes, Great Mother, I think I do! The earth gives life from what grows from it. Water gives life when we drink it, and the air gives life when we breathe it into our bodies. These three elements contain life-giving energy. When the mother cows fed their young, they were giving the life energy they received from the earth, water, and air to their calves when they drank their milk."

"Yes, my child, you are seeing the cycle of life!"

"Now, daughter, do you remember the symbols you saw on the rock?"

"I saw the four foot animals. They must represent the element of earth because they live on the land. I saw the symbol for the fish, which must represent the element of water because they live in the water, and then I saw the symbol for the bird. This must represent the element of air because the bird soars through the sky."

"Yes, now do you see why the location of the Paint Rock helps to explain the message that you said could no longer be understood?"

"Mother, you have shown me that the wisdom of our people has always been here for me to see. I only needed to see what nature was already showing me."

"Now child, you must continue to watch the men, so you can begin to understand the story your father told you."

Once the farmer and his sons made sure their cattle would be okay for the night, the time came for them to eat. They caught fish from the river, and then made a fire so they could cook them.

"What do you see?" the woman said.

"I see that the cows ate the life that came from the earth. The fish that the pale faces caught ate the worms that come from the earth, and the birds of the air must also eat the life that comes from the earth. They all eat without the use of fire—only man uses fire to eat his food!"

"Yes, child, but fire does not contain life in it, nor does it give life. It only destroys life! Man is the only one who can make fire! So, daughter; what does the symbol of man on the Paint Rock represent?"

"Fire! Man is the symbol for the element of fire!"

CHAPTER 31

The Story of the Eagle and the Owl Explained

"Did you also notice the horizontal lines that are on the Paint Rock?"

"Yes, what are they there for? These lines represent the realm of the gods. The fourth element of fire was a gift from the gods to man. The knowledge of how to make fire was only shared with man, and only he can use it. Fire was given to man to set him apart from the animals. With fire, man was given the power to create and build on the earth or to ruin and destroy the earth. The purpose of fire is not to give life like the other elements. When the purpose of fire is being used correctly, it enhances life and improves the living conditions for man on the earth, and it is here on these holy grounds that the message of the purpose of fire is forever engraved on the Paint Rock!

"The Paint Rock reminds those who make the pilgrimage to these holy grounds that fire should only be used for good. The message on the Paint Rock directs the weary traveler to the soothing waters of the hot springs. There in the water of the hot springs, man learns the true purpose for fire. Bathing in these hot pools of water shows man how all four elements can come together for good. First, the earth surrounds the pools of water. Second, the water emits the warm moist air that softens the skin and clears the lungs. Third, the rising warm air is caused by the temperature of the water. And fourth, the temperature of the water is caused by the fire that is under the earth. The four elements working together to create perfect harmony and balance!

"This is why these grounds have always been holy to our people because it is here that we learn to respect Earth Mother who provides us our food, our water, and the air that we breathe. She provides all that gives us life. And it is also here that we learn the power of the fire god. His purpose, when balanced, is to create and enhance harmony on the earth. The knowledge of the power of fire was given to man so he could learn the ways of the gods."

"Mother, I never knew these things you speak. I have only been shown the little things, but now you have shown me the great things! I'm not worthy to be your daughter, and I have brought shame to the Cherokee people. How can I ever ask for your forgiveness?"

"You are already forgiven, my child, just as your people have also been forgiven. Although, they have left the old ways and turned from the ways of peace, they were not the ones who took peace from the earth, and they are not the one who caused the elements to become unbalanced on the earth! So they will not be held responsible for the tragedy that has come upon them. That responsibility is reserved for the messenger who brought the Angry Eagle Spirit into the world. You see, your people were among the last peoples on earth who strove to maintain the balance of the elements. But the Angry Eagle Spirit has gone all throughout the world causing violence and destruction wherever it goes.

"This is why, my daughter, you have been chosen from among your people to help restore the balance. Just as your mother and father were chosen and generations before them have been chosen to make sure there will always be balance living on the earth at all times. You are now that hope for your people and for the world."

"But, Mother, I have not lived a holy life, nor have I understood these holy teachings. I have even gone against the wishes of my father and the traditions of my people by becoming a warrior, which is something a woman is not supposed to do."

"Your great love that you have for your people is the very reason why you have been chosen, and it is also the reason why you have been saved from death. Those who take life must also have life taken from them. This is one of the laws of balance! Now I think it's time that we take a good look at the story your father told you. The story that has brought you to me and me to you. This story that has given your mind so much trouble for so many days and nights.

"Now that you understand the symbols on the Paint Rock, you must use that knowledge to help you figure out the symbols of the story your father told you. But remember, in every story the symbols can change to help convey the message of the story that's being told. The wise one will be able to see each symbol for the element they represent in each story. So let's begin by thinking about the small creatures of the story. Do you remember what they were?"

"Yes, they were the mouse, rabbit, sparrow, and squirrel."

"Very good! It's clear to me that you have indeed given much thought to figuring out the meaning of this story."

"Yes, Father told me that these creatures must first be placed with the elements if I was to understand the message."

"It's good that you paid heed to his words because you have arranged the creatures in the correct order. In the story your father told you, the correct order is only given once. That was also done on purpose so you will have to concentrate on understanding the role each creature plays in the story. So for you to have already figured that much out will greatly help in bringing the meaning of the message to the surface. By using what you have learned of the symbols on the Paint Rock, how far have you come with understanding each of the elements in this story?"

"Well, two of the elements are now kind of easy for me to figure out. I think the mouse should be the element of earth because he lived in the earth. But so did the rabbit, so I'm not all the way sure about that. The sparrow, however, I'm sure is the symbol for air in the story. The problem, though, if I do have the mouse and the sparrow correct, then that would mean that the rabbit is the symbol for water and the squirrel is the symbol for fire. I don't understand how that can be correct."

"My child, this story is told in this way, with these creatures, to force the person to think about the quality and characteristics of each element. What makes earth, earth? What makes water, water? When you think about it that way, then the selection for each creature becomes clear. When we think of the ground as being earth, we think just of the few inches or so below the surface we dig to plant seeds in it. But when we think of water in the earth. we think we must dig down deep into the earth to find it. In the story, the mouse lives just below the surface of the earth, but the rabbit barrow was deep in the earth. So, yes, the mouse represents the element of earth and because water is found deep in the earth. The rabbit is the symbol for the element of water.

"Now the sparrow is the bird and birds fly through the sky, so the sparrow is the symbol for the element of air as you also saw on the Paint Rock. But why do you think the squirrel was chosen to represent the symbol for fire?"

"I don't know."

"Well, here, a little clever reasoning is needed. When you're able to use reason to help you solve problems, you become a teacher of the old ways and no longer just a student. The characteristic of fire is to burn and consume wood. The squirrel lives in the trees. Trees are made of wood, so the squirrel is the symbol for the element of fire in this story. Now if you think back to the story, you will see how each of these little creatures displayed the characteristics of each of the elements they represented in this story."

"Mother, I feel like I'm new on the earth, and I know nothing of the old ways. In one day you have taught me more knowledge and wisdom than I have ever been shown. I can't help but wonder if I should be here if I am even worthy enough to sit at your feet as your student."

"You mustn't think like that, my child. Much is going to be asked of you. You must suffer much hardship and endure much pain. Many things you are not going to understand why you must suffer through them. Other things you won't understand why you have to do them at all, but if you truly love your people, then you will do all that is required of you. You must be willing to be the light in the time of darkness so your people won't ever forget that, in the future, the time of light will return to the earth. Light is knowledge, light is balance. So for now, just try to remember that everything must be done so balance can return to the earth. However, fair or unfair it may seem to you, in you is the hope of your people and of the world.

"Now you are ready to have the meaning of the story of the eagle and the owl made plain to you, so you can understand all that has taken place on the earth and all that is to come upon the earth. The story is about the time of the beginning. The time before war and destruction was known on the earth. It was the time of the First Time! Although, this time has been forgotten and it has been erased from memory, the history of all nations, cultures, and peoples speak of this time. The time the Sky Father and Sky Mother ruled in peace and harmony. The time when the Sun ruled the day and the Moon ruled over the night.

"All the animals they created lived happily in the forest. There was beauty and abundance throughout all the kingdoms of the forest. Only one of their children became angry with selfish desires. This was the young eagle. The eagle was created to be the most magnificent of all birds, and its beauty, power, and speed was unmatched by any other creature. In its anger, it tried to change day into night and night into day. Soon all the other creatures began to become confused. They, too, stop living by the light of day, and the wisdom of the night. The anger of the eagle's spirit began to infest the realm of the forest. The creatures living in the forest became infected with the angry spirit. They all became angry, and they began to fight among themselves.

"Now, child, tell me if you understand the message of the story so far?"

"Yes, Mother, the forest is the earth, and the creatures of the forest are the children of men. But, Mother, I don't think I understand who the angry eagle is yet, and who is the owl?"

"The answers will come in time. Since you seem to understand that much about the creatures of the forest, I can now call them the children of men. First, man lived on the land, and he only used fire for its peaceful purpose. He built great kingdoms that taught all who lived in them the ways of light, which is to live in balance and peace. The people of these kingdoms lived great and wonderful lives.

"Then the Angry Eagle Spirit taught man to use fire to make weapons of war. The children of men would eventually use these weapons to kill one another on the earth. These wars lasted for many cycles of the moon and continue today. This is how the first Age of War began on the earth. It was because the Angry Eagle Spirit got into the hearts of the children of men. This was the age of the earth wars and the mouse in the story represents this time on the earth. But as the need for violence and bloodshed continued to grow in the hearts of man, he began to destroy the land. So new lands had to be found so he could continue to conquer and destroy.

"Next, the Angry Eagle Spirit thought man to use fire to make ships that could travel over the oceans to carry their warring ways out on the seas. Many of the children of men have died out on the oceans of the world, and these wars also continue today. This is the second Age of War. It is the age of the Water Wars and the rabbit in the story represent this time on the earth. You, my child, are living in the time when these two ages are upon us. The age of the Earth Wars continues, but the age of the Water Wars has already begun!

"In the time not too far into the future, the Angry Eagle Spirit will teach man to use fire to build flying machines so the children of men can take their wars to lands far away. Man will fight one another in the skies and kill one another in the skies. This will be the third Age of War. It is the age of the Air Wars, and the sparrow in the story represents this time on the earth. Finally, the last and most terrible time of war will come upon the earth. In the far future, the Angry Eagle Spirit will teach man how to unlock the secret of fire. This will be the time for much sorrow for the children of men because fire will fill the skies and many will die all at once and many more will suffer in agony from the burns on their bodies. This will be the age of the Fire Wars, and the squirrel in the story represents this time on the earth."

"Mother, your words cause my body to shake with fear. The things you speak of bring much sadness to my heart. From this day, my tears will no longer be just for my people but they will be for all people living on the earth. For those who will live during the time of fire, how sorry I feel for them. Is there nothing that can be done to stop this time from coming to the earth? Why can't this angry eagle be stopped? Tell me who this angry person is so I can go and kill him!"

"Right now, my daughter, you are the angry person. Don't you see? When you allow anger to live in you, you are allowing the Angry Eagle Spirit to live in you as well. No, to answer your question, nothing can stop the future from unfolding the way I have shown you.

"What the story is about that your father has told you is the four ages of the children of men. It is the four great kingdoms of man, and it is the four directions these kingdoms will come from on the earth—east, west, south, and north. The kingdoms that live in the final age of war will combine all the elements of the first three ages to form kingdoms that will be the most powerful and the most destructive ever to be on the earth. These kingdoms will make war on the land, on the ocean, in the air, and they will kill with fire."

"But why, Mother? why must such terrible things and such great sadness happen?"

"Daughter, I want you to try to understand for this is all that will be given for you to know. The laws that create balance create life. Once these laws are broken, death and destruction is the result."

"I still don't understand why!"

"Why is not for you to understand, but as I have already said, it is for the child that will come from you to understand."

"Then please, Mother, tell me who is the angry eagle and who is the owl of the story?"

"The eagle and the owl are not from your world. They are like me!"

CHAPTER 32

The Anointing

Willa, Wahketsi wanted to know more about the story, especially about the eagle and the owl, but she was afraid to ask any more questions. She felt, after already being given so much information, maybe it wasn't fair or wise to keep asking the Great Mother to explain more of the story to her. So she sat quietly and contemplated on all she had learned. After thinking for a long while about everything she was told, she suddenly realized that there was a question that she didn't ask, and she felt she really needed to have an answer to this question.

"Mother, why do you keep saying that a child will come from me? When I lost you, and I had to live my life always knowing that you were not in my life because of me, I vowed to never have any children of my own. I promised myself that I would never leave this earth with a child of mine having to continue living without me in their life. So how can a child come from me when I will never allow that to ever take place? If any man would even try such a thing, he would surely die!"

"I was waiting for my words to finally register with you, my little darling! Now tell me the truth—you wouldn't really kill the man, would you?"

"I would really kill the man, Mother! Before he enters me, my knife will have already entered him!"

"Oh my, but what about the cycle of life and restoring the balance!"

"These things are not of my body. These things I can do without my body being violated, Mother!"

"Unfortunately, child, I don't think it works quite that way. But you won't have to worry about such things because I know nothing like that will ever happen to you if that's not what you want to happen. So we won't talk about it anymore, okay!"

"Yes, Mother, that would be good."

After they ate soup and flat bread for the evening meal, the woman stood up and said, "This is the first chance we have had to spend time together. We should dance the friendship dance to celebrate."

"So the woman began dancing around the fire. Wahketsi looked to see if the farmers could hear her shaking the turtle shell rattlers on her feet and singing as she stamped around the fire, but the men paid no attention to what was happening right across the river from them. So Wahketsi decided that she would join in on the fun. The two of them danced and laugh for hours until they were exhausted.

"Let's sleep here by the river tonight, but tomorrow morning you must go to the cave where the hot spring is located. There, you must take another vow. You must promise that you will no longer live the way of war, and the way of the Angry Eagle Spirit. You must dedicate your life to living the way of peace, and you must be willing to walk on the path of light. Can you do this, Wahketsi?"

"Mother, when I came to you, I came here without any weapons as you asked of me. Now that you have shown me the path that leads to light, this is the path I will walk. I know now that I have been the angry eagle of the story my father told me, and I'm ashamed. I want to learn to be the wise owl like my father. Will you please teach me?"

"The path you are choosing is very difficult to follow, and there is much suffering and hardship to endure. Are you sure this is what you want?"

"All I've ever wanted was to help my people and to save our land. All the land that once belonged to your people will be taken from them, and you must allow this to happen. You can no longer resist what must take place on the earth. If I must now follow a different path in order to help my people, then I'm willing to do whatever I must."

"Good! Now if you can understand that neither your people nor the white man's people are free from the influence of the Angry Eagle Spirit, then you will see how killing one another will never solve or change the conditions that are now on the earth."

"Then what will change these things, mother?"

"The spirit that now resides in man must change!"

"How can this Angry Eagle Spirit be changed?"

"Go to sleep now, child. Tomorrow we will go to the hot springs. There you will be cleansed and your body will be purified."

"Why the hot springs, Mother? There's water here at the river. Can't I clean myself in the running water of the river? Why must we travel to this hidden cave? Why must I bathe in the hot springs?"

"Yes, in the morning, you will clean yourself in the running water of the river. You will be clean from your feet to your head. I have prepared the natural herbs soup for you to use, and when you are finished, I have special oil I have prepared to pour on your head. This is the first purification cleaning. But to be a true teacher of light, you must understand the importance of keeping the four elements in balance. You must experience this balance in your body, your heart, your mind, and in your soul. These are the four elements of man, and they correspond to the four elements of nature, earth, water, air, and fire. To bathe in the hot spring is the final step for one who is to become a teacher of light. There in the hot springs, the four elements of man and the four elements of nature combine to become one. Now go to sleep. We have much to do tomorrow!"

It was the smell of fresh fish being cooked over an open fire that woke Wahketsi from her deep sleep. As she raised her head from under the nice warm blanket, she felt the cold morning air for the first time, and it caused a shiver to run down her body. She ducked her head back under the blanket, and then peeped out from a little hole she made. She could see that the river was very calm this morning. The water appeared not to be moving at all. It almost looked like it was a sheet of glass reflecting the early morning sunlight off its surface.

THE PULL

The farmer and his sons had already moved on, and the only motion on the river bank was that of the Moon Lady. She was the only person remaining in sight of the Paint Rock, and this morning she was wearing a dress that was rustic reddish brown with matching calf-length boots. The dress and the boots had golden yellow deer fur going around the sleeves, hem, and the top of the boots. She was wearing the colors of the autumn leaves. When Wahketsi saw the Moon Lady busily preparing the morning meal, she knew that everything that happened the day before was real; that this lady was real, and that it wasn't a dream vision this time. She breathe a sigh of relief.

"Oh, I see you have come back to life! You will have a very busy day today, so I was going to let you rest a little while longer. But since you are already up, the food will be ready soon! The river water is very cold, so once you have washed yourself, you should come and be warmed by the fire. Reluctantly, Wahketsi removed herself from the warmth of the blanket and stripped herself of her clothes.

After dipping her big toe into the river, cold was not the word she thought of—freezing would have been a better word. But in spite of her momentary hesitation, she eventually submerged her feet into the ice cold water. Then she gradually walked out into the water until it was waist high. Here she could feel the river current moving just a few feet below the surface as it passed between her legs. This way, she could take care of all bodily functions before she began cleaning herself.

Once she was clean and dried, Wahketsi wrapped the bear fur blanket around her and joined her mother at the fire. There was a little clay pot with a handle and lid on it warming near the fire. The woman picked up the pot and removed the lid. Then she walked over to Wahketsi and stood behind her. She spoke words that Wahketsi could not recognize from the Cherokee language, and then she poured the warm oil on Wahketsi's head. Wahketsi could feel the warmth of the oil starting at the top of her head and slowly moving down on all sides. There was also a tingling sensation as the oil soaked into her scalp, but she didn't ask what the reason for the oil was.

"This morning meal is most important, so you are going to have roasted fish and fried eggs from the wild chicken. Oh, you should remember to thank the mother hens who allowed me to have one egg each from their nest so you can eat. I have also cooked hominy corn and made flat bread. There is also hot raspberry tea today. Doesn't all of that just sound like it's going to taste so good? I want you to eat as much as you like because this and the evening meal will be the last meals you are going to eat for a while. We have cleanse the outside of your body, and now in order to cleanse the inside of your body, you must fast. Tomorrow you will go without food. So eat as much as you like today, and after you have eaten, we are going to leave.

"I have already told Black Mist how to find the cave, and she will take us there. Don't worry, she won't take us through the river. I told her this time she can cross over on the bridge the white man has built. She will have to take us back several of the miles you came to get here to the Paint Rock. But the cave is located not too far from where the hot springs are. The last part up the trail we will have to walk ourselves. It can only be reached on foot, and that's why it has not been discovered yet.

After she was finish eating, Wahketsi got dressed. Then she made sure to pour enough water on the fire so she could be sure it was completely out. "Daughter, you have just put out the old fire of your life before. This fire was the fire of war that burned inside you all your life. When we get to where we are going, you will start a new fire. This new fire will be the fire of peace that will burn in your life going forward." Wahketsi listened to these words of the Moon Lady, and they made her feel special like she was starting her life all over again.

She then began packing everything into the blankets. "You won't need to take any of those things to the cave. Everything we will need, I have already made sure to put it there. We will wrap everything here up in the blankets and bury them in the forest. The sky is saying that snow will be coming not many days from now. We will need to make sure to stay warm as we travel up the trail, so we will take the warm blankets with us. Now we must go so we can get there in time to make all the preparations."

"What are these preparations, Mother?"

THE PULL

"You were not able to observe the Great New Moon Festival with your people because you were busy killing the soldiers."

"Yes, Mother, I know this to be true already. I didn't want to be up on the mountain celebrating the festival with my circle while those of the lowland people were being forced off their lands and being held in camps."

"Yes, I know my child, but these times of the year are important. They're not just only for times to be with your people but they are also important to keep you in balance and harmony with the movements of the heavens."

"Mother, there is so much that you understand and that I don't. I just want to keep quiet from showing my ignorance."

"It's okay, little young one. Others had to learn just as you must now learn. Even though you missed the Great New Moon Festival, and even though it's a little late for the Cementation Festival, we still must have a holy celebration for your coronation as a light teacher. Since it's never too late to make new friends, we are doing a slightly different version of the four days Cementation Festival.

"On our first evening together, we danced the friendship dance. This morning you were purified in the running water of the river and the oil was poured on your head. Tomorrow you will fast all day, and on the fourth day, you will be purified in the hot springs. Then you will dance the friendship dance with your new friend. He will not need to come to the Paint Rock, so he will join us on the last night at the cave. Besides, he has needed all this time to travel the distance on foot to get to where we will be."

"What new friend, Mother? You and I have already danced the friendship dance."

"His name means 'light giving.' In the heavens, it is the sun that lovingly gives its light to the moon so she can light man's way through the darkness. He will be the sun to your moon, and you two will create balance. He has never taken human life, so he will be made pure in the waters too, and you will help teach him the way of light. My child, I want you to remember the words of our people, 'A woman's highest calling is to lead a man to his soul so as to unite him with source. A man's highest calling is to protect woman so she is free to walk the earth unharmed.'"

"I do not know the Cherokee name for light giving, Mother. Who is this man?"

"He will be your new friend, dear!"

CHAPTER 33

A Hidden Secret in the Forest

Luke had been walking for days now on the trail that took him through the mountains. Since the first day when he saw the white deer following the creek up the mountainside, he has only stopped to rest at night. After the first night when he had to sleep behind a boulder so he could be hidden from the path; he has since fallen asleep wherever he has been able to find a comfortable place to lay his head. It was on the second day of walking that he finally reached the first water pool just before evening. There he could see that someone had recently stopped. The same horseshoe prints were in the mud around the watering pool and over by a tree. There was a sunken area in the grass that showed someone had lain in the grass to rest or perhaps to sleep for a while.

He decided that this would be where he would spend his second night on the trail because he knew that this is where the woman on the horse stopped to get a drink of water and to rest, or at least this is what he had convinced himself to believe. The nights were starting to get colder, and although he had his blanket roll with him, he felt that he would have to risk starting a fire just so he could keep warm during the night. Also, the beef jerky was not going to last much longer and he had to find something to eat. While he was thinking about what to eat, he heard the frogs around the watering pool begin to make their mating calls for the evening. He remembered the time that he tried eating frog legs for the first time. It was at the officer's dinner party that was given for the cadets after their graduation ceremony.

That night, he had Mary Beth Belmont on his arm. She was the daughter of Captain Belmont, who was his father's best friend. These two men had come up through the academy together, and they had both married daughters of military men. It was just naturally assumed that he and Mary Beth would eventually get marry too. He even heard his father, and Captain Belmont discussing it once. They seemed to be very pleased with the idea. Now there was nothing wrong with Mary Beth; she was a very fine young woman. But with them growing up together and playing together as kids, she always seemed more like a sister to him than someone he would fall in love with.

It's true, though, since they hadn't seen each other for almost ten years because when she turned fifteen, her parents sent her away to boarding school. She did look quite different. She was certainly not the skinny little girl he remembered growing up. She was now a fully developed woman, and she was very attractive. She would make a fine wife for some lucky guy someday, he thought, but to him, she was still Mary Beth.

Maybe it was just the fact that her hair was also blond that made it hard for him to see her as anything more than just a sister. When he looked at her, it was almost like looking at himself. This may not have been a problem for his father and Captain Belmont because they both married women with blond hair. But for Luke, it felt like he would be doing just what was expected of him and that he wouldn't really be doing what he felt was in his heart.

To get away from that situation was another reason why he left home to come to the South. He thought that he just needed to take some time to clear his head before making such an important decision. Now he finds himself on a mountain trail in Georgia following after a mysterious woman who tried to kill him the first time he saw her. What would his family think of him if they knew that this Cherokee woman made him feel more alive in that brief moment they spent together then all the years he spent with Mary Beth? Would they understand that the woman a man falls in love

THE PULL

with should make him feel like there was a purpose for them meeting each other. He already knew what his father would say to such talk. "Son, you have a great career ahead of you in the Army. With the right woman as your wife, it can only help to open doors for you." And if he was to be honest with himself, it wasn't too long ago that he felt the same way.

So he couldn't blame his family if they didn't understand the decisions he has been making lately. He didn't really understand why he was out there looking for this woman either. He just knew that if he ever was going to understand what happened that night between them; then he was going to have to find her. He did worry, however, how his recent behavior would affect his mother. Will she somehow blame herself for him not following in his father's footsteps? He knew that once his actions are discovered; he would be considered a deserter and a trader. He didn't want his mother to suffer on his account.

Mothers always seem to take the blame for the perceived failures of their children. Not only that but his mother really liked Mary Beth. She and Mary Beth have always gotten along very well together. She said Mary Beth was the daughter she never had. This did make him feel that it would break his mother's heart if she found out that he left the Army to find a Cherokee woman to be his wife. Enough with the thinking like that, I'm not even sure I will ever see her again, and I already have us married. Let me go see if I can catch some of these frogs so I can have something hot to eat for dinner.

To Luke's surprise and disbelief, the frogs didn't jump into the pond upon his approach. They actually allowed him to pick them up. This had to be one of the strangest things he had ever seen. It was right up there with seeing a white deer come out of nowhere and then disappear back into nowhere. But be that as it may, he was going to have frog legs to eat for dinner that night, and this made him happy!

Early the next morning, he was able to wash up in the pond and fill his canteen with fresh water, so he could start, as early as possible, back on the trail that he believed would lead him to Wahketsi. He walked all day and didn't stop to rest until the sun was starting to set for the evening. Then the next day he did the same thing all over again.

Wahketsi helped her mother onto Black Mist's back. She handed her the two warm blankets, and then she jumped on too. Her horse didn't wait for a command but started the trek back towards the hot springs just as the Moon Lady said she would.

"Mother, in order to get to the cave, won't we have to travel past the hot springs where the pale faces will be this time of morning? When I came this way, I had to make certain that it was so early that the sun had not come up yet. But the sun has already been up for hours and we are just now leaving."

"Yes, but the way Black Mist will take us, she will keep us hidden in the forest, and she will avoid making contact with any strangers. This way will take a little longer then traveling on the trial, but we should still get there in plenty of time to prepare the wood for the ceremonial fire for the last night. After we take care of that, you have to decide what it is you would like to eat for the evening meal tonight. You will have to hunt for the food, so you should make sure it's something you can carry back by yourself.

"I think it should also go well with beans, corn, wild potatoes, and greens. So keep that in mind, too, while you are looking for our food. Oh, it would also be nice if you would have already cleaned it before you bringing it back."

"Yes, Mother, turkeys are gathering for the winter cold this time of the year. I will bring you back a young male turkey ready to roast on the fire."

"That would be excellent!"

It was around midday when Black Mist reached the spot where she couldn't travel any further up the trail. The steep hill that would take them to the cave had large rocks protruding out of it side that almost looked like they were placed there by a giant. These ten very large rocks zigzag up the hill, and they were mostly round on the bottom side but flat on the top side. The rocks looked like they could be used as steps for this giant to walk up the steep slope with ease.

Wahketsi wondered if this hidden cave they would be going to didn't once belonged to the giant people. She wanted to say something to her mother, but she didn't want to appear afraid. Somehow, the Moon Lady knew what she was thinking. "Don't worry, child, the time of the giants has long past on the earth. All that is left of them are old bones and some of the caves they use to live in. So you don't have anything to worry about, and don't worry about Black Mist either; she will be okay here. No harm will come to her. I will take the blankets and start up the hill. Tie her up and then follow after me."

As she tried to climb up the hill, Wahketsi began to understand why this cave had not been discovered. It was nearly impossible to get your footing without slipping on the green yellowish moss covering the hillside. The only time you had solid footing was when you managed to reach one of the large rocks protruding out of the hillside. But Wahketsi noticed that the Moon Lady didn't seem to have any problem, whatsoever, climbing up the hill. She wondered why she was able to walk up the hill without slipping when she wasn't.

That's when she noticed that the Moon Lady was walking diagonally from one rock to the next, and each time she reached a rock she would wiped her feet on the rock before she continued. She, however, was trying to walk straight up the hill, and this is why she was having such difficulty. So after studying what she saw the Moon Lady doing, Wahketsi started moving up the hill sideways, walking from one rock to the next. When she tried moving up the hill this way, she discovered, to her surprise, that hidden beneath the moss were groves in the soil that allowed your feet to walk up the hill without slipping as long as you walked from one rock to the next. To keep the moss from building up on the bottom of her moccasins; she also had to wipe her feet on the rocks once she reached them.

Wahketsi wondered why her mother didn't tell her about the groves hidden under the moss. She didn't think it was fair that she let her slip and slide back down the hill so many times without telling her what she was doing wrong. Although she felt frustration when she finally reached the top of the hill, she didn't say anything to her mother because she understood that this was a test that she had to figure out on her own. She thought about the words the Moon Lady spoke when she said that once she started to use reason to solve problems, she would become a teacher of the old ways. Although her clothes were now stained green and yellow from the moss, she still felt proud of her accomplishment. Also she couldn't help but noticed that the Moon Lady was staring at her moss stained clothes with a slight grin on her face.

Finally, after walking for a few hours through brier patches, thick bushes, and low hanging branches from trees that, had it been summer when they were covered with leaves, would have made it impossible to see away to past the thick brush. But Wahketsi could see that there was a clearing coming up ahead. Because there was so much of this thick over growth blocking the way to the cave; she thought that the only time of the year one could reach this cave would be in the spring or the fall. It would be impossible to attempt to climb that hill once the winter snow had fallen.

Once they cleared the brush, they walked out in front of what appeared to be a wall made of the same rock material found on the hill, but the golden yellow stones that made up the wall were polished and very smooth. Again, the look of amazement came over Wahketsi's face, so the Moon Lady began to explain the wall to her. There are twelve of these giant rock slabs that formed the wall that encased the entrance into the cave. There are three slabs on each side of the seven foot opening into the court yard in front of the cave, and three slabs that turned on right angles at the end of the front two walls to form a perfect square shape enclosure for the court yard of the cave.

Each one of these slabs stands seven feet high and seven feet wide and are two and a half feet in thickness. This makes the front wall, including the seven-foot opening, to be forty-nine feet across. The exterior of the two side walls are twenty-three and a half feet long. These stones looked enormous to Wahketsi, and she thought they would have been extremely difficult to move and put into place. These giant slabs seem to have been placed in this manner to keep the forest from encroaching on the cave, and the forest seemed to have obeyed their command. The overgrowth stopped well short of reaching the wall. There were no low hanging tree branches near the wall; no bushes or tall grass came anywhere close to the wall either, and the wall, itself, was free of any type of growing vines.

THE PULL

Once they walked through the opening in the wall, the Moon Lady began pointing out to Wahketsi the design of the courtyard. The floor of the court yard was made from polished granite that was of an emerald-green color with specks of gold coloring in them. This was the first time Wahketsi heard the word granite, and she realized, in that moment, that the giant rock slabs that made up the wall was also granite.

From one side of the courtyard to the other side measures forty-six feet, the Moon Lady explained as she continued describing the courtyard to Wahketsi. Someone, she said, laid these huge granite slabs using the same method that was used to move and to put the granite slabs of the wall into place, and they did it using precise measurements. Wahketsi thought the Moon Lady knew who that someone was that built the wall and courtyard, but she didn't say anything.

In the center of the courtyard is the circle of granite rocks. The circle, which is seven feet in diameter and in alignment with the seven foot entrance into the courtyard, is made up of nineteen smaller rocks that are also golden yellow in color with the smooth polished finish like the wall. The outside of the circle measures nineteen feet to each of the side walls of the courtyard. In the middle of the circle is the only place on the court yard floor that isn't covered with the granite. The earth remains within the circle so wood for the ceremonial fire can burn there. Now eleven feet from the center of the circle is the entrance to the court yard, and eleven feet in the opposite direction is the entrance to the cave. As you can see, the entrance to the cave is huge; from the ground to the ceiling it measures twenty-nine feet in height.

Wahketsi could not believe her eyes. She thought they were going to some little cave on the side of a mountain trail. She had no idea that she was being taken to a place like this. She remembered, as a little girl growing up on the mountain, the many stories that were told to the children about the great things those who were of the First Time had built. She remembered the stories that told of their great knowledge and magical powers to move stones great in size, and then shape these huge stones to form mountains, and to build great and wonderful kingdoms. But she never thought she would actually get to see one of them with her own eyes.

"This truly is no ordinary cave, Mother! This place is a holy place. This cave is a temple built to the gods of the First Time!"

CHAPTER 34

Wahketsi: The New Star

The day of fasting was finally coming to an end. Wahketsi had not eaten since the evening meal of the day before, and the sun was finally setting on this difficult and uncomfortable day. To just say that she was hungry would not be telling the whole story. She was also awfully thirsty; she had not drunk any water since the day before either, and she felt like if she did not die first from thirst, she was going to starve to death. She was ready to eat and drink as much as she could.

Her mother had made turkey soup from the turkey meat that was leftover from the turkey she caught. She had started simmering the broth for the soup very early that morning. Wahketsi had watched her put carrots, onions, celery, green peppers, and lentils in the soup. All the cooking was done outside of the courtyard but still the smell from the soup cooking all day filled the courtyard anyway. There was nowhere Wahketsi could go to avoid it. This only made her watch the movement of the sun more closely than she ever did before. *Sun, please hurry up and go down!* Wahketsi prayed.

Even though when the time came to eat, she had already drunk two cups of water, she still drank the first bowl of hot soup straight down. Yes, the soup burned her throat a little as it when down, but it tasted so good. The next bowl she managed to dip some flat bread in the soup and chew the turkey meat a little more. Then she was able to pay attention to the roasted potatoes and seasoned cooked greens. She ate as much as her stomach could hold, and then she decided to stop for a while. The Moon Lady only had a bowl of the turkey soup and a cup of the hot tea.

After an hour had passed, Wahketsi decided to take a walk through the forest so she could bring comfort to her stomach. When she returned to the courtyard, the Moon Lady was waiting.

"Child, soon it will be time for you to enter the cave and bathe in the waters of the hot springs. Once you have entered the cave, you must drink from the cup filled with the drink of sight. Then you must remove all your clothing before entering the water. You must remain in the soothing waters until your animal spirits appear to you.

"Each animal spirit will represent one of the elements, and these elements will correspond to the elements of your body. Remember, the animal of earth will be your new body. The animal of water will be your new heart. The animal of air will be your new mind, and the animal of fire will be for the new soul. With these new totems you will learn to master the elements and become a true teacher of the way of light. You must also allow them to guide you on the journey you must take from here.

"I also have a gift for you that I would like to show you before you enter the cave, but you can only wear it after you have come from the cave, and after you have started the new fire in the holy circle, and danced around the circle of fire seven times. The gift from the Moon Lady was a white deerskin dress made similar to the one she wore the first day Wahketsi saw her; only it had embroidery of colorful beads going around the collar, sleeves, and hem. There was also white deerskin boots with the same embroidery at the top. Her mother also gave her a waist-length white rabbit fur jacket to go along with the dress and boots. "Mother, everything is so beautiful! They will be here when you come from the cave and finished your dance. Now the time has come for you to enter the cave."

Wahketsi had not entered the cave before now because the Moon Lady told her she could only enter the cave once the time came for her to bathe in the water of the hot spring. Even though it was starting to get late into the evening, it was approaching the seventh hour of the night, there was light coming from somewhere in the cave that made it possible to follow the path down to the pool.

THE PULL

The cave floor was made of the earth, and the dirt path was compacted like it had been walked on for many years. The walls and ceiling of the cave was made out of the same green granite, and with the gold specks in the granite sparkling from the faint light, it looked to Wahketsi like she was walking among the stars in the heavens above. As she continued down the path to the pool, Wahketsi thought to herself that if what the Moon Lady say is true then, it is the old person walking down, but I will be a new person when I walk back up this path.

When she reached the hot spring, she saw a new pair of moccasins and a new loin cloth and another cloth to dry herself once she came out of the water. There were also two turtle shell rattlers for her to wear when she danced. Next to these things was the cup she was to drink from. All these things were placed on a ledge that had been shaped out of the rock wall of the cave. Wahketsi drank the liquid, and then she removed her clothes and slowly lowered herself into the nice warm water.

After only a few minutes of sitting in the water, she began talking out loud to herself. "Mother was right, the water is very soothing, and I can feel my skin softening as I sit here. The moist air is even softening my hair, and my breathing is so clear. Why am I talking to myself? Why do I hear my own voice when I'm not talking to myself? Then she noticed an animal figure standing at the edge of the pool. Why is the she-wolf I heard the night I left the camp staring at me? Why am I not afraid?"

"I have come to you," the she-wolf began to speak, "to bring courage, intelligence, and the love of freedom to your body, and now I will enter the water." Then the she-wolf disappeared into the water. Then she heard the sound the frog makes, and there was the frog sitting on the earth in front of the pool too. "Why are you here?" Wahketsi asked. "I have come to you to bring strength in the time of change to bring love and fertility and the ancient wisdom to your heart, and now I will also enter the water." Then the frog disappeared into the water.

"Now I see the crow that had awakened me when I fell asleep by the watering pool. Why are you here?"

"I have come to you to bring your destiny, powerful magic and transformation abilities to your mind, and now I will enter the water." The crow disappeared.

"What is this ball of fire hovering over the pool of water that I see?" When the ball of fire opened its wings, Wahketsi could see that it was a bird made out of fire. "What are you?"

"I am called the fire bird, the Bennu, and goddess of the wing disk, but those from your people have also called me the Thunderbird. I have come to you to bring rebirth and the resurrection to your soul, and now I will enter the water." It, too, disappeared into the water.

When Wahketsi awakened, she was still sitting in the hot spring pool, and that's when she realized she had another dream vision. *But was that real? Did these animals really come to me, spoke to me, and did I also speak to them? Did they join with me as the Moon Lady said they would?* Then she realized that she had no way of knowing how long she was asleep, or how long she has kept her mother waiting.

She quickly got out of the water, dried herself off, placed the loin cloth between her legs, and then raised it in the front and in the back. Then she tied the band around her waist and let the excess cloth material fall back down in the front and in the back. This made the traditional Cherokee loincloth almost appear to be a short skirt. She then hurriedly put the turtle shell rattlers on each ankle and slipped her feet into the new moccasins.

When she walked from the cave, topless, with only the loincloth for clothing, she did not see her mother anywhere. There was a stick with fire burning on one end resting against one of the rocks of the small circle of stones. Inside the circle was the wood she and the Moon Lady had stack up for the fire dance. With her body starting to get cold, Wahketsi lit the fire with the stick that was there and started to dance. As she danced around the circle with the noise coming from the rattlers on each ankle, her body motions began to move in rhythm to each stamp of her feet. Slowly at first she moved around the fire, and then a little faster as the noise coming from the rattlers got louder and louder. Until, there she was, dancing in the dark wearing only a loincloth. Then as she danced, she started to sing the songs of the friendship dance.

THE PULL

The dancing was making her body temperature rise, and she was getting warmer. Soon, droplets of perspiration were forming on her body, and her bare breasts and skin began to glisten from the light of the fire. As she turned herself in circles as she danced around the fire, she began feeling the way she felt that night in the tent. Once more she danced around the fire—four! Once more she felt her heart beat increase—five! Once more she felt the sensation of that night get even stronger—six! Once more her body temperature became even warmer until perspiration now covered her entire exposed body. With every movement of her body, the light coming from the fire was reflecting off her moist glistening skin as if it was now her dance partner.

The warmth of the fire, the rhythmic motion of her body, the sound of her voice echoing off the granite stone walls of the court yard, and the sound coming from the constant stamping of the turtle shells on her feet was enthralling. Just as she was beginning to be carried away by the euphoria she was feeling, that's when she saw him—seven!

Standing there in the entrance to the courtyard, staring at her nearly naked body, was the Ghost Spirit. The only man that ever met her knife and she didn't kill. The only man she could never kill!

Willa, I going to end this letter here because I want to take some time to talk to you about everything the Moon Lady said to our ancestor Wahketsi. We are the children that the Moon Lady promised Wahketsi would come from her. I'm telling you, our family history because I want you to know this burden we have carried from generation to generation. I have waited up until before I thought you were ready to hear these things about us. I also know how hard it must be for you to believe they are true, and I don't expect much for you to believe everything I'm writing to you now. When the Stranger comes to you for the first time, then you may be ready to accept what I have to say.

But you should know some of these things ahead of time, and that's why I'm telling you the ancient history of our family first.

Once I finish telling you the story of Wahketsi, you should finally be ready to hear the story of how your father and I met. We met during the ending Age of Water because the Age of Air had just now started. You are now living in them times the Moon Lady called the Age of the Air Wars. Willa, this means that your children will be living in the Age of Fire! This is something that has troubled me greatly for a long time. So I'm not sure if I should have waited until you were a little older or not. You haven't even met your husband yet.

Willa, even though, you may have a hard time believing this story. I think it will be mighty helpful if you study everything the Moon Lady said to Wahketsi. If I was you, I would read the whole story over several times if you have to just to make sure you understand everything she revealed to Wahketsi. I can promise you something though; you won't be understanding everything the first few times you read it. It has taken me most of my life to finally understand, and I regret that when I was younger I didn't believe these things. Because I can already see the same things are happening to you that happened to me.

Time will tell if I have made the right decision because what you do to prepare your child for what is coming to the earth will depend on how well I'm able to explain everything to you to the best of my abilities, and maybe you won't make the same mistakes I made. I can only hope that we get this right.

In the next letter I write to you, I will finish telling you what happened that night on the mountain in front of the cave when Wahketsi and Luke saw each other again.

With all my love, Mom!

ABOUT THE AUTHOR

Ralph Nathanial Wells was born on March 7, 1957, in Sumter County, South Carolina.

At the very early age nineteen, the author realized his special passion for discovery. Having read all the childhood mystery novels like *The Hardy Boys, Nancy Drew, Sherlock Holmes*, and many others, he began his own research work that would take him the better part of twenty-five years to complete.

His chosen fields were history (ancient and modern), world religions, the Bible, science as it related to the fields of his research, and a host of other subjects. After accumulating a substantial amount of material and information, he discovered that research papers weren't very interesting to read and were seen by most as just plain boring.

This is when he decided to take this wealth of knowledge he had gathered from basically all over the world and create something that was completed different and new—a novel series that combines history, religion, and science in such a way that it would be a challenge to find any such attempt ever being tried before.

The first book, *The Pull*, in this amazing series will open the eyes and mind in such a way that the readers' view on American History will be forever changed. The story of the Cherokee people's place in our history has never been treated with such detail, compassion, and respect. Theirs is a story that you will definitely want to read.

CPSIA information can be obtained
at www.ICGtesting.com
Printed in the USA
BVHW03*1009250618
519965BV00007B/77/P